*

Wild Waters in the Roar

*

by
Mike Noel-Smith

authorHOUSE®

AuthorHouse™ UK Ltd.
500 Avebury Boulevard
Central Milton Keynes, MK9 2BE
www.authorhouse.co.uk
Phone: 08001974150

© *2008 Mike Noel-Smith. All rights reserved.*

No part of this book may be reproduced, stored in a retrieval system, or transmitted by any means without the written permission of the author.

First published by AuthorHouse 7/23/2008

ISBN: 978-1-4389-0420-7 (sc)
ISBN: 978-1-4343-9861-1 (hc)

Printed in the United States of America
Bloomington, Indiana

This book is printed on acid-free paper.

This book is for anyone who is bold enough to dream but, through no fault of their own, cannot realise that dream. Remember, there is always tomorrow…

Dedicated and in memory to my parents

*

ACKNOWLEDGMENTS

*

This book could not have been written had Rob and I not undertook this amazing passage in our lives and I have to thank Rob for coming up with the idea in the first place. Once committed to rowing the Indian Ocean we experienced overwhelming support before, during and after. It is impossible to mention everyone and I apologize right now if I have missed someone out, but we would like publicly to thank the following, in no particular order.

To our families who not only believed in us throughout, but helped us financially, emotionally and spiritually. To Kate Abernethy for designing and running our website which kept so many people following our voyage and contributing to our charity. To my brother Denis for being a rock throughout and to Clare and Bibi for helping with fundraising. To my father Ron, Robs parents Desmond and Liz, my parents-in-law John and Di for having the faith, Buffy's sister Sue and her husband Simon for fundraising in Germany even after we had been rescued!

Friends too many to mention, but you know who you are, and you know what you did by keeping us amused during our row with emails or phone calls, helping before we left but more importantly, helping Buffy and the children when, to coin a phrase 'it all went horribly wrong' and your fantastic support on our return. A big thank you.

To a huge support team, Chris Cherrington our Project Director back in the UK for seeing the project through and organising our return. To the 'Admiral' Bill Black our coach and mentor - thank you for all those painful gym sessions and constant words of wisdom. To Lee Bruce and Rick Friswell for supplying our weather data and forecasts before and during the journey. To Peter Moore, without your help and patience in lending us the boat none of this would have taken place. Huge thanks must go to Stuart Ross whose diligent and professional help with PR and Media gave us the exposure that we needed as well as your very kind help towards Buffy out in Australia.

To everyone at SPARKS in particular John Shanley the CEO, Paul Connew – Head of Communications and Helen Farquharson – Head of Fundraising. Your work continues to be an inspiration to so many and we were very proud to have represented your charity and in particular, Dr Kathy Triantafillou at the University of Portsmouth.

To Scipio, the person who will not be named but whose interventions, support, trust and friendship will be an example to us in our lifetime. Words cannot describe how we feel about you, but of course you know that! We gave you the name Scipio because it best sums up you with what this legendary Roman General achieved in his own lifetime: a brilliant and brave strategist, a leader who encouraged others to 'think outside the box', someone who understands the value of determination and training, but above all, someone who makes things happen! This and more you gave to us, and we will never forget that.

A huge thank you to HMAS Newcastle, the CO Captain Gerry Christian, the Executive Officer Steve Hughes, the Weapons Officer Steve Gibson, Lt Sue Sharpe and her assistants in the medical bay, Kingsley, Sue and Sam and all crew members who came to our aid out there in the wilds of the Indian Ocean. Your professionalism, dedication and humour throughout your mission to 'come and get us' will never be forgotten by Rob and I, nor indeed our families and friends who watched the events unfold. It is with pride that we can say we knew you. To John and Ruth at Vivid Agenda, whose diligence and professionalism helped me complete the book. My grateful thanks.

In addition to those remarks above here is a list of our Sponsors who all helped in one way or another, again thank you for your faith in the project and your support. In no particular order they are:

Betfair (our title sponsors) in particular Mark Davies, Head of Marketing, and Stuart Ross, Head of TRANSVenture PR and Media
Bad Vodka Jelly
Little Dewchurch Church of England Primary School
Aussie Bodies
Garmin
Holmes Place Fitness Gym, Monmouth School Gymnasium,
Kudos Vitamins
Wheelhouse Creative

Yahoo!
SkyWest Australian Airlines
Best Western Hospitality Hotels
Transas Navigator, Satamatics, Fleetviewonline
X Glue London
Sprint Physiotherapy Ltd
Sysmedia
Cathay Pacific
British Olympic Medical Centre
Richard Large and P&O for getting the boat back
Paul Chapman at SmithKline Beecham for the Lucozade energy drinks
Tactical Weather and Lee Bruce
Australian Bureau of Metrology
Carnarvon Sea Rescue
Challenger World

Finally, to Buffy and my children William, Isabelle and Harry. My love and admiration for you all has grown throughout this adventure. I know that I put you through a lot, and yet you always came out understanding and smiling despite the difficult times. You are a strong team and I am proud to be called your husband and father. Of course, you will probably have to go through it all again…

CONTENTS

*

Prologue		xv
Chapter 1	'See You In Reunion!'	1
Chapter 2	You Don't Need A Weatherman...	21
Chapter 3	Hard Work	37
Chapter 4	Mind Games	53
Chapter 5	Magic	69
Chapter 6	Tide of Fortune	81
Chapter 7	Disaster	91
Chapter 8	Incredible Things	95
Chapter 9	Waiting	101
Chapter 10	Rescue	113
Chapter 11	Epilogue	123
Appendix 1	Glossary of Terms	131
Appendix 2	Fitness and Nutrition	135
Appendix 3	Poems We Recieved at Sea	147

Over 2000 yachtsmen and women have raced around the globe
1,312 mountaineers have summited Everest
188 explorers have reached the South Pole
450 people have been into space
12 people have walked on the moon
No team has ever rowed unassisted across the Indian Ocean...

*

PROLOGUE

*

"It is curious how much I have a sense of the nearness of disaster and danger…the sea is as deeply evil as it is attractive"
(George Mallory, 1921 on route to India from Tilbury aboard the SS Sardinia in the Indian Ocean).

DAY 41 – Friday 31st May
Location: 23:07:745S 91:25:974E distance covered: 1631nm

Two men in a boat. OK, it was a rowing boat, but apart from that, our adventure bore little resemblance to Jerome K Jerome's comic masterpiece. Rob and I weren't pootling down the Thames – we were over 1,700 miles out into the Indian Ocean, in the middle of a violent storm that was quite outside our worst nightmares. Three men would have been useful.

We were rowing from Western Australia to Africa and outside our survival cabin the wind howled and the waves pounded the sides of our boat TRANSVenture.

We lay in our stern cabin ironically called the 'coffin' dozing in and out of sleep. Condensation dripped from the ceiling and mixed with the sweat drenching our clothes. We were constantly jolted from side to side. It was like a screen theme park cinema, where the seats move to the motion of the film and there is absolutely nothing you can do to stop the 'ride'. We both felt helpless, but a desire to keep our macho counsel stopped us from discussing our fear. It was only later, when we were safely home that we admitted how scary and claustrophobic the coffin was just then. We were cowering from the storm in a space that was just 6 foot 2 inches long by 4 wide at its widest end, tapering down to 2 foot at the back of the boat. The roof was only 3 foot off the floor – sitting upright was laughable.

I hated being in this tiny place, not being able to see outside properly and listening to the noise of the sea bashing the side of the boat, the maniacal rattling of our small wind direction flag outside and the occasional heavy thump as water crashed onto the deck itself.

We had expected bad weather after our 'met' update some 12 hours previously. We had battened down against the forecasted 25 knots of wind and up to 7 metres of swell. Unfortunately for us, the weather system bearing down on us exceeded our worst fears and we were gripped by a violent storm that raged for another 24 hours.

Eight thousand miles away in the USA, our trusty weatherman, Lee Bruce studied satellite photography and foresaw the approaching nautical nightmare. He tried calling our satellite telephone, but we had switched it off to save power. He called our project director in the UK to see if he could warn us, and finally, unbelievably in the circumstances, he tried to reach us by email. What he saw on the satellite was pretty bad – gusts topping 40 knots and ocean swell increasing to 9 metres. In short, a tropical cyclone. That's a dangerous, unpredictable weather system by anybody's book, even the most experienced and well-equipped of sailors.

Our 21 foot rowing boat was about to be put through a grueling test of its seaworthiness. Tony Bullimore, a vastly experienced round-the-world yachtsman suffered conditions like these in the Southern Ocean off the coast of Australia several years before our row. The result was a complete capsize of his boat (three times the size of our craft), irreparable damage and a massive rescue operation to save him from drowning.

A huge wave rushed in on us like a steam train. There was a second of silence followed by an enormous crash that lifted all ¾ tonnes of vessel off the ocean and smashed her back down with a large 'crump'. I said to Rob, "That's a big one!" He responded with a characteristic shrug. But within a minute we both realised something was drastically wrong as we took a number of wave blows to the side and rear of the boat. Had the unthinkable happened – the wave ripped the sea anchor from the bow of TRANSVenture and with it some of the bow section itself? If so, we would soon start sinking…

With a hollow feeling in my stomach and heart pounding I opened the watertight cabin hatch and crawled out onto the deck. I tried to ignore the awful pain in my head from my accident earlier that evening. The only light was from my head torch. I emerged into a watery hell with waves crashing over the boat and the wind whipping the sea into a white frothy fury. Clipping my harness onto the decking supports I crawled to the far end to see what damage had been done. It was the longest, most terrifying five minutes of my life as I crawled just twelve feet from the stern to the bow end of the boat. I was constantly being submerged in cold water as wave upon wave washed over the decks. It was difficult to breathe without taking in great gulps of salty water.

To my astonishment, the bow section of the boat was intact – but there was no sign of the sea anchor. My brain struggled to take it in. For a bizarre second I thought that Rob had somehow managed to unclip the anchor and pull it in for safe keeping. How could 2.5 tonnes of high tensile steel shackle snap and take with it 75 metres of 13 mm reinforced Kevlar rope, strong enough to tow a double decker bus? The horrible realisation that the anchor had really gone suddenly brought me down to earth. We had to tackle the problem in hand – stabilising the boat before we were capsized by ever larger waves. I crawled back to the cabin to fetch Rob.

As we struggled to deploy the spare anchor we were hit again with a massive force that tilted the boat through 60 degrees. I found myself half in the water gripping the oar gates to stop myself being washed overboard. Without the stability of the sea anchor, we were helpless victims of an ocean that seemed bent on toying with us – and very close to disaster. Finally, weighed down by Rob's precious shotgun, the spare anchor slipped into the heaving seas and started to bring the bow of the boat into relative safety.

Back in the cabin, we began coming to terms with our frightening experience of the massive power of nature.

*

CHAPTER ONE
'SEE YOU IN REUNION!'

*

"Man cannot discover new oceans until he has courage to lose sight of the shore"
Anon

ON BOARD OFFICIAL DIARY
DAY 1 – Easter Sunday 20th April
Location: 24:29:406S, 112:42:158E distance covered: 44nm

Our journey began at Kok's point on a rocky, uninhabited piece of coastline guarding the entrance into Shark Bay in the northern part of Western Australia. It was just before midnight – a beautiful clear night with a star studded sky and a deep inky black Indian Ocean below. The boat felt tiny compared to the ocean all around us. The next time we saw land would be 6000 kilometres later, on the large volcanic island of La Reunion off the Eastern coast of Africa.

As we moved further into the ocean, the sound of waves crashing behind us against the coastline became ever-softening 'crumps'. After only two or three strokes into the journey of a million such strokes I lost sight of the twinkling cabin light in the tow boat. The distant sound of Rick and Chris calling out "good luck lads, see you in Reunion" was swallowed up in the darkness. We were truly on our own for the first time. For a split second I wondered what we had let ourselves in for. The intensity of the next few moments was quite overwhelming. I was gripped with the anticipation of a young child stepping fearlessly out into the world, mixed with adult feelings of hope and trepidation about what lay ahead

The only interruption to the peace of that first night was the sound of our oars slapping the surface of the water and the occasional grunt as we propelled our 1-ton boat TRANSVenture. We didn't utter a single word in those first five hours. But our brains worked as hard as our muscles.

Transventure in Carnarvon with all our stores ready to be packed into the hull. Fully laden she would weigh over 1 ton.

I thought how privileged I felt to be taking on this massive challenge with Rob, carrying our own hopes along with those of everyone at home who had supported us. I thought about the scale of the journey and the weather ahead, and what kind of routine we would need to get into. And even though we were just hours into a trip that would last for months I also thought about matching Rob's performance stroke for stroke. I didn't want to let him down and he was younger, bigger and stronger. I'd had to work hard to get to a comparable level of fitness and I wanted him to have faith in me. I thought too about how I would look after my 'baby' the boat, today and for the rest of the journey. I'd spent a great deal of time cleaning, varnishing and painting her in the last six months at my home. As we rowed on, my mind buzzed and crowded with a thousand thoughts – how were we doing, how far had we gone, when would it get light, who was going to make breakfast, what was that fish jumping in the dark out there? I recalled the day twelve months back when Rob called to say that he wanted to row the Indian Ocean.

"Hi Mike, Rob. Ever wished you'd done something – you know – epic?"

"Rob, every day is epic if you think about it. What the hell are you talking about?"

"Look, I'm 30. I'm bored. So I've decided to do something epic with my life".

"Great, just let me know when you get back then," I humoured him.

"No mate, I'm going to row across the Indian Ocean from Dar es Salaam to Jakarta and I want you to come."

"Are you mad? You've never rowed before or been to sea for that matter. Anyway what about all the girls you'll leave behind, what on earth will they do without you?"

"I'm serious, check out ocean rowing on the web."

"You're crazy. Ok, ok. But can you finish that job that I asked you to do last week before you go please?"

He was barking mad, I told myself.

But then I went over and looked at my wall atlas. And despite myself, I did some internet research and then I realised that it was a challenge I couldn't resist. Rob probably knew that too.

Although many had rowed the Atlantic and the Pacific, no Britons had successfully taken on the Indian Ocean. The recognised route was from Australia to any point in Africa, including Reunion Island, east of Madagascar. Pictures of beautiful tropical beaches and palm trees filled my mind.

I've always felt my life has been lucky – more adventurous than many. Maybe it's in the genes: my father was a fighter pilot in the Second World War. I served in the British Army, spending several years at the sharp end of the Northern Ireland 'troubles'. Then I led 350 men to the top of Monte Bianco in the Italian Alps, became the first person to ski down the Mexican volcano Popocapetl and worked as a film stuntman, simulating a suicide jump from 600 feet from one of the tallest buildings in Berlin.

This rowing trip would be an epic one and, at 45, I decided I couldn't let the chance pass me by. I'd put the idea to Buffy. We've been married for 20 years, and she has always been calm about my sometimes crazy notions.

Ocean rowing was something that neither Rob nor I knew anything about. I vaguely remembered from my childhood in the Sixties that Chay Blyth and John Ridgeway, two serving Paratroopers, had completed a sea journey that caught the nation's imagination. They'd crossed the Atlantic in a tiny open-decked rowing boat. When I searched under 'ocean rowing' on the internet, an enormous amount of information came up. It was a serious endurance sport.

Rowers were racing across the Atlantic in organised competitions. People had rowed the Pacific, of all things. This was seriously interesting!

I looked up details for the Indian Ocean and discovered that it had only been crossed successfully once before, way back in 1971, by a lone Swede called Anders Svedlund. I started to get excited. No British rowers, and more importantly, no pair or team in the world had done this route. I also quickly discovered that Rob's intended path from Africa to Indonesia was flawed. Not only was it the wrong way to go in terms of wind and current, but it would not count as a recognised route. The Ocean Rowing Society, who appeared to be the fount of all knowledge, had labelled the Indian Ocean route as any point from Australia to a point on the African continent, including a small island called Réunion just to the East of Madagascar.

My mind screamed out "go on, have a go"! I had never rowed before at school or in the Army, but surely it couldn't be that difficult? As for the sea, currents and wind, again that must just be a matter of picking up the knowledge? I dashed downstairs, found Buffy outside in the garden and told her my idea.

Buffy writes: 'When Mike asked should he go, I gave what is my standard reply to most of his ideas, "Fine". I can't understand why people have asked me about this so many times. Did they really think that Mike would go off without my blessing? I must admit the huge task ahead didn't dawn on me immediately. But from the start I gave Mike all my support, including trying to help him follow the strict diet he needed to get fit. As the months of training went by, I saw his body transformed to the one I'd first known! It was a delight and a very pleasing by-product of his hard work.

To be honest, I'm not sure how I really felt about the trip. It was something that Mike felt he needed to do and he's a free spirit, so I felt honoured to let him fly – that's the best way of putting it.

I have a strong family and group of friends around me, supporting Mike and me. When I confided in people, there were no worried looks or gasps, only acceptance and support. This backed my belief that this was part of Mike's path. Christina, one of my very close friends is psychic and she felt the same as me; this trip was part of his journey through this life."

Mike: My biggest worry at this point was my back. I'd seriously damaged it during my time in the Army. I'd fallen out of a helicopter and then injured it again during a crunching tackle in a rugby game. Rowing I guessed was pretty much the last thing my lower back would appreciate, but hell, you're only on this planet once. Once I'd made up my mind, that was it and all I had to do was to tell Rob that I was coming along with him. I had no doubts about going with him. Anyone would choose him as their partner in an adventure. He gives his all in whatever he sets out to do and somehow he always keeps his sense of humour. We had worked together for some time and understood each other completely. I also knew he was very strong physically, a distinct advantage for the journey we were about to set out on.

I phoned him back and told him I'd be coming along:

"You really can't go on your own, mate. First, you'd go mad. Second, you'll definitely need an older and wiser head there with you. And third, we're a great team already. We can do this!"

At first, we kept our plans to ourselves. I did not want to worry Buffy's parents and my father, who would probably think I was mad until I'd proved to him that all the bases were covered. Rob was also concerned about how his parents would react. He'd just completed an MBA and been in full time employment for only a year.

But I decided very early on to tell my children. They needed to share in the dream. William, Isabelle and Harry arrived home from school that day and were pretty amazed at the news. Harry, the youngest at 10, thought it was a great adventure straight out of a comic book. Isabelle and William, both teenagers, agreed it would be an epic voyage but wasn't I perhaps a little too old? When I explained that the whole family would have to go out to the remote island of Reunion in the Indian Ocean for a reconnaissance and holiday, they became far more receptive to the idea.

Rob and I were overtaken by a huge wave of enthusiasm as we began delving into the ins and outs of ocean rowing. We felt we'd make a great team; in fact we'd already proved it, working for Challenger World, a firm that delivers large team building events for companies. We had similar backgrounds and a mutual respect. We'd both served with the British Army, Rob with the Brigade of Ghurkhas and I with the Gloucestershire Regiment. We were both rugby players, representing both the Army and Combined Services. We had a determination to succeed, experience, humour and a willingness to get the job done. These attributes would stand us in good stead over the next year of preparation for our adventure.

DAY 2 – Easter Monday 21st April
Location: 24:40:400S, 112:20:225E distance covered: 75nm

The pinks, yellows and oranges of our first dawn on the Indian Ocean rose magnificently behind us and the air temperature increased quickly. In front of me, I could see that Rob's back was already streaked with sweat and salt, his biceps bulging as he leant into the next stroke. Light broke with a host of sea birds hanging on the breeze some 20 feet or so off our stern. A constant 'caw caw' filled the air as they jockeyed for position, hoping we were a fishing boat with scraps to throw over the side. A hundred yards over to the starboard side a school of flying fish were chased by a large shoal of dorado, the flashes of colour blurring through the water as the life or death struggle took place beneath the waves. A small turtle, oblivious, trundled past us through the water heading back to the land.

The coastline was still visible, but a healthy distance away now as we tried to escape its smudgy and dangerous outline. I remembered Sir Chay Blyth's wisdom before we left, "lads the most dangerous time for you on this trip will be the start and finish. Getting smashed to pieces on the rocks is a strong possibility, so row hard at the start and be cautious at the end"

Finally, at eight o'clock with the temperature up at 30 degrees, Rob slid his oars in through the gates and stretched. "Right, a really good start, you crack on rowing and I'll get breakfast on". Soon the smell of strong coffee filtered through the sea breeze and down into my nose, nudging my taste buds. It seemed like a long time since I'd begun rowing. I got out of my seat and stretched. Rob handed me a big black mug of steaming coffee and we both washed down a couple of energy bars and some macadamia nuts. It was a meagre breakfast but all that our bodies & minds wanted. We were high on adrenaline, and already felt there was no time to lose. So after a very jittery pee over the side, I quickly began rowing again.

As I pushed on our westerly course across the ever- increasing swell, I could feel my UV screen shirt and long trousers sticking to me. I wiped the salt and sweat from my face and glanced down at my watch to find that the temperature gauge read 36 degrees. And it was still only ten o'clock in the morning. Happily though, it was time for Rob to take over and my grateful body crawled off the seat and into the cabin for some rest.

With the forward hatch open and the sun beaming in I felt satisfied with our start and content with the world. But despite the gently rocking of the boat, I couldn't sleep. At that point I didn't care. The trip seemed too much like good fun to miss. We had a quick lunch because we were too excited to cook anything properly. More fluids and crunchy bars were enough.

As the sun sank lower into the horizon, the weather began to worsen. The swell became more pronounced and waves slapped the side of the boat with more force than in the afternoon. Darkness descended suddenly on the ocean and our small place on it.

"Rob, switch on the mast light will you, and get my head torch out of my bag".

I was beginning to feel vulnerable after being jolted off my seat a few times with waves that I could not see as they arrived to crash against the boat. The mast light came on and bathed the small deck in a weak glow, hardly improving the situation, but it felt good to have it. It made me feel reassured that everything was fine.

Rob crawled out of the coffin with my head torch.

"Bloody hell, this looks a bit shitty, what do you reckon?".

"I think we need to stop and get the sea anchor out for perhaps a couple of hours just to see if this is going to blow through".

I wasn't particularly happy, suggesting this to Rob. I was afraid he'd think I was scared. Which I was. But I also felt that it was dangerous to carry on rowing.

To my relief Rob said, "Definitely, let's stop for a while."

Great, I was glad he felt the same way. Happily, we were able to spend the whole trip in this amicable way, despite the hardships and hazards. We had decided this well before we set off, while on a training trip to Lake Windermere in Cumbria. In the hotel bar, I reminded Rob of some more good advice we'd had from Chay Blyth. He said we needed a set of ground rules if we were to avoid falling out in a tiny boat while at sea for months.

Rob said, "I think it's a good idea, not that we will have problems. But anyway, it's still worth writing down a list of our values I guess."

I grabbed a beer mat and borrowed the barman's biro.

This is the list I scribbled.

1. We will have fun.
2. We will be honest with each other all the way and in everything we do.
3. We will not have arguments; arguments are futile and time wasting, so we won't have any.
4. We will respect each other's point of view.
5. We will train as hard as we can.
6. We will smile and have a laugh every day, whatever.
7. We will succeed.

Well, we pretty much achieved six of them. The seventh was the tricky one.

I was looking forward to using the sea anchor for the first time. Rob took over rowing to keep the boat head into the wind while I crawled up front where the bag containing the sea anchor was tied onto the deck. It was simple: I chucked the bag containing the parachute and its weight into the briny. Once in the water, the parachute inside the bag would unfurl and become a parachute, slowing our boat down and turning the bow into the waves. I prayed silently as the white marker buoy bobbed off into the darkness that it would work properly with no snagging of the myriad wires and lines that held the parachute.

Within a couple of minutes I felt TRANSVenture turn into the waves, pulled by the underwater parachute 80 metres in front. I crawled around the deck with my head torch on to check that everything was well and truly strapped down and then sat contentedly outside the cabin seeing and feeling how the boat performed in the building swell. All seemed well, so I crawled into the cabin – or 'coffin' as we soon took to calling it, and joined Rob.

The word 'cabin' conjures up an image of a nice snug place to relax on board ship. But the inside of an ocean rowing cabin is quite the most uncomfortable space to try and sleep, read, work or pray in. As you entered our tiny cabin on the right hand side was the electrical panel to power the mast light, GPS, tracking beacon, laptop computer, water-maker, satellite phone and marine batteries. Alongside the electrical panel was a small handheld fire extinguisher and a fog horn. My 'bed' was on this side. Very soon into the journey I realised that I had drawn the short straw, as all these hard items had a habit of sticking into my back, ribs, head and various other parts of the body. Opposite were a couple of shelf units and drawers housing the nautical maps, log books and manuals – most notably the water-maker manual. This area was designated a 'water free' area, so no changing out of wet clothes. This was Rob's 'bed'. No more roomy than mine, but at least it did not have metal objects sticking out from the cabin sides. Lucky bugger.

The size of our small cabin made doing the simple things difficult. Here Rob is trying to work out where we are

The floor was covered with camping mats that were stuck down on top of the marine plywood to give our bodies a little protection. Underneath the floor was the better part of 3 weeks worth of meal bags, stored in bins. Towards the centre of the cabin where it started to narrow either side, we had a length of string bags containing spare t-shirts, a couple of towels each, books, mini disk players and torches. These bulged alarmingly as we tried to squeeze more and more items in. At the end where it was narrowest we had out first aid bag attached to a couple of bungee cords. There was a small but powerful light on the roof section, because although we had 2 hatches these did not give much light inside.

We decided to have another pull on the oars again at around midnight. The moon was up, like a huge searchlight on the ocean. Beautiful, but it was a complete waste of time trying to row. If anything, the swell was building rather than dropping off. Rob spoke briefly to Chris, our project director on the satellite phone with our first sit rep (situation report).

We kept this to a standard format throughout our trip so that calls were brief but did not miss anything out – must have been a throw back to our old Army days.

We covered:

- Ocean state – direction of wave and swell, height of wave and swell, direction and strength of wind, day temperature
- Distance and bearing (direction) covered in past 24 hours and location
- Personal state – how we felt, our general morale, any injuries and what medical remedies/steps we were taking
- Wildlife – anything we had seen (so this could be put onto our website for the schools that were following our progress)
- Requests - to be sent to family and friends

This was our first report:

"Hi Chris, Rob here, with situation report number 1.

Ocean state - Swell and wave coming from the South East, Swell height 2 metres and breaking, Wind gusting 15 knots from the South. Wind appears to be building. Highest temperature, 34 degrees. Twenty-four hour measure 44 nautical miles, bearing 180 degrees, Location: 24:29:406S, 112:42:158E

We're both well and strong, no sleep yet.

Plenty of sea birds following us still; we saw one green turtle and we think a sailfish jumping 100 metres from the boat

Tell everyone we are well, having a great time and just glad to be away from the coast – and had wonderful spaghetti bolognaise for supper. We've had to stop for the time being as the conditions at night are too bad to row, so we are having some time off in the coffin."

Around one in the morning, the active radar alarm went off indicating a vessel within 10 miles. Excited, we both got out on deck to have a look. I spotted some distant lights and tried to work out if the vessel was coming towards us. I hoped not. It's extremely difficult to judge distance in the dark at sea, and a collision was always a real possibility when a boat came near at night. We had heard of incidents where the officer in charge had simply put the ship on auto-pilot and gone off to have supper or play cards, while his 30,000 tonne vessel ploughed through the night. Our only defence would have been to fire flares and to keep calling up an international radio channel that all ships were supposed to be listening out on.

Training in Shark Bay with the Carnarvon fishing fleet in the background

Rob was convinced he could hear dolphins in the dark somewhere, but every time he said "listen over there", the noises disappeared. I hoped this was not the first sign of madness.

It turned out to be a bloody awful night. I closed the hatch on the wild winds buffeting the boat from all sides and we both tried to settle down in the cramped conditions. It was impossible to get comfortable as we jolted from side to side. It must have been well past 3 in the morning when exhaustion finally dragged me into sleep.

★

DAY 3 – Tuesday 22nd April
Location: 24:31:275S, 112:07:969E distance covered: 93nm

We start rowing again at 0700 hrs after a quick brew. I was sick again and could not eat my cereal. During the bumpy night my nausea had turned to vomiting and liquids were the only thing I could stomach. I threw my water bottles away – the bottom of them was coated in a nasty sludge that I couldn't rinse out. We had plenty of other smaller water bottles so they were no real loss. For the first time since leaving Australia, we got into our two hours on, two hours off routine. Rob spotted a large container ship off our starboard side, probably coming out of either Geraldton or Fremantle. I tried calling it on our VHF radio to alert them that we were there but they didn't answer.

"Hello, unknown container vessel steaming approximately North North East at 24:31:275S, 112:07:969E, this is TRANSVenture on your port side heading due West. We are a 21 foot rowing boat bound for Reunion Island, Africa. Do you see us on radar, we are active on Channel 16. Over."

I repeated this two or three times, and then gave up, finishing with:

"Hello, unknown container vessel this is ocean rowing boat TRANSVenture, nothing heard out."

Thankfully, it disappeared over the horizon without coming any nearer.

As I took over from Rob mid morning, I saw a dark shadow on our port side – our first shark, a bronze whaler about seven feet long. It seemed curious rather than hostile and after a couple of laps around the boat it disappeared into the depths.

There was no wind to speak of and it became very hot around midday. My temperature gauge read 43 degrees, hot enough to leave our 'boil in the bag' meals on the deck to heat through! Well, it saved on gas. Within 20 minutes they were ready to be eaten. I managed to keep this meal down, which was a good thing as I needed to build up the fluids I'd lost through sickness and pure sweat.

We were definitely up against the Leuwin current by this point. As the day wore on, we could see from the GPS that all we were doing was 'holding station'– in other words going nowhere. After six hours of rowing in the blistering heat we'd done precisely 1.1 nautical miles – very depressing. To combat this we tried rowing both of us together for four hours but this made little difference. At 2330 hrs we gave up, put the sea anchor out and prepared for yet another cramped night in the cabin. To take my mind off our dispiriting lack of progress, I put on my headphones and lost myself in Dire Straits. Then there was a nudge from Rob. He wanted to borrow one of my mini discs. "Yeah, no problem." This is when I found out Rob only had ONE mini disc with him. He'd been listening to Meatloaf's 'Bat out of Hell' for days; now I knew why. He was lucky that I had gone to the other extreme and meticulously recorded eighty hours worth of tapes especially for the times when there was nothing else to do.

The highlight of the evening was my call home. I spoke to Buffy and Will – very good for morale. The line was so clear it felt like they were standing beside me.

"Hi darling, it's me, how are things?"

"Hey wow, you sound so close, how are you?"

"Yep, this satellite line is great. We're fine, but we're battling the elements a bit. It's much harder than I thought – the waves and wind are trying hard to take us off! How are the kids?"

"Everyone is very well, but your website positioning chart isn't working so we haven't a clue where you are. How far have you gone, what's it like rowing at night, how's your bottom?"

"Hey, too many questions! I don't have that long on the phone. We've done about 100 miles and my bottom is fine thanks – those special padded seats are great. Night rowing is cool providing we have a moon to see the waves, otherwise it gets pretty scary."

"Here's Will."

"Hey my boy, how's school?"

"Hi Daddy, school is fine although revision is boring. Miss you lots, Daddy"

"Miss you too my boy, but we are going along well. Got to dash, can you hand me back to Mummy please, take care?"

"Bye sweetie, got to go as I've had my ration of minutes. Give the other two a big hug from me, and have one yourself. Love you"

"Love you too, row hard, we are all very proud of you. Take care of yourselves. Bye for now."

I'd mentally prepared myself for being away from the family for a long time, but this first contact reminded me how much I loved and missed them. It was hard.

I put my earphones back on and my mind drifted back to when Rob and I first got together to lay our plans.

Rob came down from London to my home at Pool Farm in Hertfordshire one weekend in early June. As we sat on the village green discussing the project, we quickly realised there was a huge amount to do and that we would have to give up working for Challenger World. Rob is very 'bullish' and positive and was confident we would get a major sponsor to take care of our incomes during training and preparation. With three children, two of them at fee-paying schools, I had to ensure there was money coming in every month. Rob lived in Fulham and would also need to continue to pay the bills.

Our quest began over a lunch with Ben Taylor, the International Sponsorship Manager for Orange. He advised to put our plans into a pitch document to present to companies. He was also quick to point out that the sponsorship market was very tough and that we should be prepared for a long haul and many disappointments. Companies needed to see a clear benefit to any sponsorship contract, whether it was promoting a new brand, exploiting a new market area or even energizing a tired workforce. They would not simply chuck money at us just because _we_ thought it was a great project.

We started at the top, targeting big companies with a track record of sponsoring nautical adventures and races. Over the weeks and months we got a steady barrage of rejections. Most dispiriting were those that didn't bother to reply to our letters. But some of those who did cheered us up a little.

"We are sure that you will have delightful time, but are sorry we cannot support your holiday."

"We agree when you tell us that more people have flown in space than have rowed the Indian Ocean – unfortunately this is also exactly the same number of projects we have sponsored in our company's history."

"As a company we are focusing more on supporting our staff in helping them to achieve personal goals. Not even our staff would be crazy enough to attempt such a daunting voyage, but we wish you every success."

"I wish you every success with your unassisted row across the Indian Ocean – I sincerely hope you survive (!), and I am sure that you will raise lots of money for your charity."

Next, we consulted some eminent people who'd raised money for marine adventures, starting with Sir Chay Blyth whom we visited in Gloucestershire. It's fair to say he didn't waste time giving us false hope. He warned us that getting sponsorship would be the most difficult part of the project. His advice was to organise a cocktail party at home and invite all the local big wigs to listen to our plans over a glass of sherry. That way we might be able to link into the local community and perhaps generate a number of small sponsors rather than just seeking the 'big one'. We were not enthused by this idea one little bit. We truly felt that if we could find the right synergy with a company, our enthusiasm and determination would take us through to get the money.

We approached over 350 companies without success. We had 87 meetings, mainly in the City, and spent countless hours on the telephone.

By mid August, we had no sponsor, no boat and we were both due to give up our jobs in under a month's time. Things looked very bleak indeed…

✭

DAY 4 – Wednesday 23rd April
Location: 24:21:798S, 112:02:710E distance covered: 117nm

Dawn, and after a good hearty breakfast we cracked on again but only made 1.5 knots in very thick sea that Rob had dubbed 'porridge'. We were caught up in an eddy system and the water was backing up on itself. The monotony of rowing was broken up by the fantastic passing entertainment – shoals of tuna chasing flying fish. It was far better than watching a David Attenborough documentary and we had ring side seats. On my rest period standing in the 'well', colourful butterflies fluttered around us – a startling sight so far out to sea.

The container ship 'Clipper' passed us bound for Darwin and this time I managed to make radio contact.

"Hello container ship Clipper this is ocean rowing boat TRANSVenture off your starboard bow transmitting on Channel 16. We have you active on our radar, do you see us. Over"

"Hello TRANSVenture, this is Clipper bound for Darwin, we have you visual at 1600 metres. We had radar contact at six nautical miles. How big are you and where are you going? Over"

"Hello Clipper, we are rowing from Carnarvon to Reunion Island off the coast of Africa. We are a 21 foot marine plywood rowing boat. We have been at sea only for three days. Over"

"Hello TRANSVenture, from the sound of your voice you must be Poms! You are faced with an enormous journey; I hope the elements are kind to you and your tiny craft. Do you need anything from us? Over"

"Hello Clipper. Yes we are British. Thank you for your kind words and no thanks we do not need anything, I was just interested to see whether you had registered us on your radar, and you have answered that question. Thanks for the chat and cheerio. This is TRANSVenture, over and out"

"Hello TRANSVenture. Roger that and all the best of luck. You truly are mad. This is Clipper, over and out"

We maintained the two hours on and two hours off, day and night to try to get away from the coastal current and eddy systems. According to Rick back at the weather station in Carnarvon there was some bad weather coming in that could be with us for the next four days. Despite this news we were rewarded with a stunning sunset. I took some photographs with Rob's body silhouetted against a backdrop of purples, violets, pinks and gold. Fantastic!

A good sleep quickly became something that our bodies ached for. We both had experience of sleeping 'rough' in the Army. In fact, I used to pride myself on being able to get some shut- eye pretty much anywhere. From Observation Posts (OP's) dug into farmers' manure mounds around Europe to icy snow holes in the Alps and wet flooded jungle river banks in Belize, I've had my fair share of uncomfortable places. Rob confessed to sleeping in fly infested huts in the Himalayas, beaches in Hawaii and alleyways behind pubs in Fulham! But hands on hearts, sleeping in the 'coffin' that was our survival cabin on an ocean rowing boat wash the most uncomfortable of all. We were in a space of around six and a half feet by four feet; fine for one person. But with two people, not only did it get a shade too intimate, it also got extremely tight.

Next to no ventilation was the second problem. If we dared to sleep with the hatch open to catch the breeze, there was the risk of the ocean joining us without warning at some point. Rob and I got thoroughly soaked very quickly into the voyage. The other drawback of an open hatch was that it compromised the self- righting ability of the boat and you turned turtle, with the risk that the boat would not right itself. So the hatch mostly stayed shut.

Third problem was that the boat moved constantly, gently rocking or manically bouncing about. Either way your body followed the boat's motion. On your own and with some careful propping of clothes (often wet) against the body, you just might stop yourself sliding from side to side. With two of you, it was bedlam, and more like a good rugby ruck with arms, legs and elbows everywhere.

One last element that made for less than perfect slumber was the padding that we had lovingly applied to the floor of the cabin back in England. The camping 'carry mats' were absolutely fine on a dead calm day but turned into torture mats capable of giving friction burns to hips, elbows and knees when the boat rolled about. To combat this we had to wrap vulnerable body parts in our few spare clothes, but even then there was some serious chafing. It all added up to concentrated sleep deprivation after the first week. Astonishingly, our bodies began to shut out the pain and fatigue after a while – survival is a very strong instinct!

★

DAY 5 – Thursday 24th April
Location: 24:03:761S, 111:35:230E distance covered: 151nm

With the arrival of dawn we saw from the GPS that we had put over 150 nautical miles between us and Kok's Point. Both of us were exhausted with the 24 hour rowing shifts. I'd kept myself going with the belief that our bodies were simply trying to get used to this cruel and unusual punishment. None of the rigorous physical preparation work could replicate what we were now feeling in our shoulders, arms, legs and bodies. Every sore or chafe was a cause for concern. Our hands were calloused and they hurt for the first five minutes of rowing until the soggy mash of flesh beneath our gloves warmed up. Blisters were forming on blisters, but we both knew that given time, they would harden up.

The wind started to pick up so we 'parked' up for breakfast and did some personal hygiene, which consisted of washing our bodies down with clean water and tee-shirts with salt. Then I set off on the oars again heading WNW. The winds started to die around 1000 to more manageable stuff of around 10-12 knots but in the back of our minds was Rick's gloomy forecast of 25 knots of wind and 6 metres of swell. Rob gave Chris our sitrep and it appeared that our tracking beacon in the forward cabin was not working. Satamatics back in the UK could not track us as they were supposed to, and neither could family and friends. It explained the conversation that I'd had with Buffy a couple of days previously.

I crawled up to the forward cabin. The suitcase-sized piece of kit was loaded with electronics and a mini-computer, a sort of 'black box', like the type found on aircraft. Short of checking the connections there was nothing much that I could do. The apparatus appeared to be ok, so I hoped it was a fault at their end that could be fixed quickly.

I didn't appreciate it at the time, but this faulty piece of equipment was causing all sorts of dismay and concerns back at home. Buffy had tried to find out where we were on the web, and was unable to – it looked for all the world like we had just disappeared. My mate Nick spoke to Fleetview Online, the providers of the graphic display to get some solutions. He tried to explain to them that the morale of our families and friends was seriously affected by not being able to see any progress by the intrepid rowers. It took several days to sort out. It turned out to be a technical problem in the UK and absolutely nothing we were doing or had done on the Indian Ocean.

Buffy:" The tracking system had been causing me great frustration as our internet access provider didn't allow me to view their progress. Friends kept calling me with updates and yet, at home on the computer I couldn't see a damn thing. I contacted both Transas and Satamatics for help, but the man I needed to speak to was away. Then the phone rang and it was Transas asking if I knew what was happening with Rob and Mike. I thought *they* were meant to tell *me*! They had lost their ability to track them. My head went into a swirl, as Transas explained it could be down to the size of the waves and that I was not to panic but contact them as soon as I heard anything. I knew that if the boys had a problem, their SOS would go direct to Chris but I couldn't get hold of him – he was on his way back from Australia. 'Keep calm everything will be fine' I kept telling myself'.

Mike: Rob gave up his oars and crawled into the cabin. Newly inspired, I took my turn at pulling. I pushed on into the blustery night until 2230 hrs when a wave hit us violently broadside on, and we pitched so far over I thought we were going to turn turtle. Rob had a rude awakening as he was hurtled across the cabin. That was it. His head emerged from the cabin hatch window, cursing. He suggested putting the sea anchor out again to keep us into the waves. I didn't argue. The weather got steadily worse during the night and for the first time I was worried about the ability of our little boat to take the hammering from the waves. We lay, bored and sore in the cramped cabin. We would both have much preferred to be outside rowing, despite the storm.

DAY 6 – Friday 25th April
Location: 23:53:015S, 111:21:250E distance covered: 171nm

As the sun came up, the weather was still terrible with swells of up to five metres and incessant waves. Sitting into the waves on the sea anchor in these conditions reminded me of being on a roller coaster ride at an amusement park – but out there it wasn't funny. I called up Rick on the sat phone and he gave us the glad news that the conditions would almost certainly worsen over the next four days. With over 2000 miles ahead of us, there was nothing to do but try to row to get some mileage under our belts. Anything was better than being cooped up in the cabin. As Rob began rowing, an enormous billfish (probably a marlin) flew right out of the water and crashed down about 70 metres away from our boat. It was a most amazing sight, repeated seconds later, only much closer. We could even see the water streaming off the powerful body of the fish as its long black spear-like nose defied gravity for a second before crashing back down and disappearing into the depths with a huge swirl. I couldn't help feeling sorry for its prey – probably the large school of tuna that had been worrying the smaller flying fish earlier.

Then a big container ship appeared on our portside. I tried to make radio contact, but they didn't answer despite being only about a mile away. An uneasy feeling gripped us; we had heard back in Carnarvon that quite often the bigger vessels were driven only by a computer while the crew played cards below decks. A vessel plunging through the night with nobody on lookout duty could quite easily mow us down without even realising. My mind drifted back to a story Dom Mee had told me. He'd been hit while rowing with Tim Welford across the Pacific Ocean, and they were extremely lucky to have survived the incident. A fishing vessel ran them over despite Dom and Tim firing flares, radioing and frantically shining lights. Rob and I were luckier. The container ship ploughed on through the waves like the Mary Celeste and away from us.

During the afternoon I mentally bet with myself on which of the approaching waves would break on to the deck. It was great when I gauged it right. I could quickly slip the oars on to the deck and hold on to the sides.

The waves I misjudged were painful. If I left an oar in the water, my arm and shoulders were jarred painfully as I fought to save it from the crashing water.

By 1900 hrs the wind was increasing again so we decided to stop and put out the anchor. I delayed going below, and sat alone in the well on deck with my harness strapped to the jackstays, watching the ocean whip herself up. I leant into the cabin and could hear Rob's deepened breathing. At least he was finally getting some much-needed rest.

My thoughts returned to home; during our phone call I discovered that Buffy had broken into the world of media. This is how she recounts her first radio interview:

'Hereford and Worcester Radio called and asked if I would talk on air about Mike's progress after four days on the ocean. I had to chuckle to myself – me, doing a live radio interview! The limelight was the last thing I wanted. I'd dodged Mike's media launch in London by taking the children to a pottery workshop. But this time, the drive to support Mike and SPARKS overcame my own thoughts and desires. I dropped Izzy and Will off for the school bus and then went on to leave Harry at school early, so that I could get to the studio. Time keeping has never been one of my virtues, I don't wear a watch and am often early before I set off somewhere but frequently arrive late. But by a miracle or just pure determination I was early for my first radio interview. I sounded squeaky, like Pinky and Perky, the TV puppets from the Sixties. Words that normally flew to my lips were lost in the deepest recesses of my mind. Thankfully, the radio presenters carried me through. A friend who's normally technophobic even recorded it for me!"

Mike: I received a great email from Nick back home: 'Hi boys. Arses like baboons yet? Found a clipping from the Aberdeen Evening Express which I thought might brighten your day: *At the height of the gale, the harbourmaster radioed a coastguard on the spot and asked him to estimate the wind speed. He replied sorry, but he didn't have a gauge. However, if it was any help, the wind had just blown his Land Rover off the cliff'.*

*

CHAPTER TWO
YOU DON'T NEED A WEATHERMAN...

*

*"Where a dreadful storm it did arise,
and the stormy wind did blow"*
Sea Shanty by John Renfro Davies

DAY 7 – Saturday 26th April
Location: 23:35:180S, 111:04:575E distance covered: 191nm

The combination of a rolling boat, thundering waves and the rank smell from our unwashed bodies made for another awful night. I found it difficult to sleep because I wasn't getting enough exercise and was worrying about our slow progress. Rob and I tentatively discussed our concerns. We were only a week into the trip but we could have walked further in the time. At 0730 hours I started to wrest the sea anchor from the thrashing waters. It took about 15 minutes of heaving and groaning before I managed to stow it away. Several times I nearly lost my fingers as the swell 'gave' me line and then snatched it back with frightening speed. This was the worst sea we'd seen, with the swell way over 5 metres and high winds whipping spray into our faces. Through the day we watched a pair of oceanic white tip sharks lurk about 10 metres away on our port side. If the swell broke we could be joined by half a ton of angry fish. I estimated that they were around 10 foot long and they seemed drawn to us. We thought perhaps the watermaker was making acoustic noises underwater that mimicked a distressed fish. The sharks' unblinking, soulless eyes looked primeval, and added to my feelings of insecurity when I crawled on to the deck.

When I called Rick, our adviser at the Australian Metrological Department, he warned that the storms were likely to be with us for six days. His predictions got worse by the day. Perhaps he was hedging his bets. It was disheartening news, meaning we'd need some exceptionally good conditions to get back on target and complete our voyage in 64 days. I took the precaution of attaching a stronger rope to the spare sea anchor and called home to update Buffy and Harry. He just wanted to hear stories of the monsters we'd seen and the fish we'd caught.

"Daddy when are you going to send photographs of sharks, how many have you seen, have you shot at them yet, how big are they…?"

Throughout the voyage, Harry was fascinated by the sharks and the questions came tumbling out. He was also very aware that his school was following the row every day, and wanted some 'inside' information to tell his mates in the playground.

We kept rowing until 1730 hrs when we could no longer see the incoming waves, and put out the anchor. Another worry: our tracking beacon still wasn't sending out signals.

★

DAY 8 – Sunday 27th April
Location: 23:32:400S, 110:52:800E distance covered: 199nm

Dawn brought more tempests. We didn't know if we could do anything in these wild seas, with the winds blowing up to 25 knots. Our weather router Lee Bruce called from the USA to say that his models showed the swell had reached six metres during the night and the weather wouldn't improve for days. We watched the perilous swell – a strangely magnificent sight - gather momentum and height. TRANSVenture climbed up the waves for a few seconds until we crested the summit and saw miles of water for just a few moments before crashing down into the trough. Then it began again. We were majestic at the top, insignificant at the bottom.

We left our oars tied up on deck and, as the light faded, I put out our second anchor to see if it made us more stable. It was a long shot - making no difference except to sap my energy and leave me soaked to the skin. Lee called again to encourage us, saying that at least we were only on the fringes of a storm that was much worse to our South. We avoided talking about our frustration at not being able to row through the day and night. But we felt impotent as we were thrown about in the coffin like rag dolls. Rob kept on poking his head out of the hatch window, willing the weather to improve. To drown out the rushing waves I played Jimi Hendrix on my mini disc player at full blast. 'All Along the Watchtower' was apt: "…and the wind begins to howl."

Cooped up in the coffin, I remembered how we finally acquired the TRANSVenture. It was more difficult than I had expected. After six months of futile enquiries, I'd begun to feel desperate. Without an ocean rowing boat, all our planning and training would come to nothing. We phoned around the world but everything was either sold or beyond our budget. I remembered several times getting up in the middle of the night and going to see if anyone had responded to my pleading emails. So it was a godsend when Ali Cockayne came up with her idea.

Ali is one of the loveliest ladies I know. I first met her when I worked with her then-partner, the former England rugby captain Will Carling. She struck me not only as very beautiful but also warm hearted, with genuine empathy for people. She's Gary Linaker's sister-in-law, and so moves in celebrity circles, but she's one of the least pretentious and kindest people you could meet. She was great fun to be around, with a huge smile and child-like giggle. It was a great shame that her relationship with Will finished in the way it did, leaving her heartbroken. She came and stayed with us in Hereford for two weeks with her little son Henry. We gave them as much love and support as we could in their difficult time and I am delighted that she is now happily married.

Ali said that we should approach David Ross, the co-founder of the CarPhone Warehouse. The company had already sponsored two people who had rowed across the Atlantic. Ali spoke to David and then called me with the fantastic news that he was willing to help us. Without Ali we would not have secured the boat and I am eternally grateful to her.

I spoke to Peter Moore who, with Scott Gilchrist, had rowed the boat across the Atlantic the previous year. He was really supportive and understood our predicament - no money and no boat - and he agreed to let us hire his.

On a bright, crisp winter morning Buffy and I travelled down to Windsor to meet Rob and Peter and collect the boat. It was the first time that Rob and I had actually been on one and we clambered excitedly all over the deck. She looked a little sad sitting on her trailer with flat tyres and her deck covered with autumn leaves - but she was a real ocean rowing boat, not someone's poncy gin palace. Buffy went to Slough to get a pump for the tyres and some trailer lights while, over lunch, Peter gave us a run-down on the equipment, what we would need to replace, and tips on how to row. We really felt that our goal was in sight now, as we pulled out of the yard with the 21-foot boat on the tow hook. Back home, I failed to appreciate the scale of the turning circle on 28 feet of trailer as I clipped the ancient wall leading into our drive, demolishing two metres of stone that had stood for 300 years. It gave me much more respect for caravan drivers…

We decided to call our baby the TRANSVenture (The **Rob Abernethy Noel-Smith VENTURE**) and we were very proud of her. We quickly had to get her out on to the water and see if we really could row together. We had four months left and a lot of sea training to do. I'd done a bit of sailing, some windsurfing and a little white water canoeing, but nothing substantial. The only time I had spent a night on the sea was on the Poole to Cherbourg ferry.

Over the next few weeks our boat lived in the barn while we cleaned her and prepared for our first trip out on the water. I left home at 2am on a cold December's morning for the long trip north to the Lake District and our first major rowing expedition. We were both excited and apprehensive, unsure about so many things: could we steer, how heavy would the boat be, would we sink? It was a freezing cold day with grey scudding clouds and drizzle when our coach Bill Black met us with his customary smile and wink.

We first met Bill through our work on team-building events where he acted as the arbiter in disputes. He is tall, silver haired and built like a combined long-distance swimmer and cyclist. Quietly spoken and witty, Bill had been the personal coach to many top athletes including the World Triathlete champion Spencer Smith and the Great Britain Triathlete squad coach at the Sydney 2000 Olympics.

With Bill standing in the 'well' like Admiral Nelson, we took our first stokes in an ocean rowing boat. Very quickly we knew there was something wrong. Why were we going so slowly? Lesson number one: ocean rowing boats weigh up to ¾ of a ton and a little like a super tanker, they take a long time to get going. After much grunting and swearing we started to move slowly but surely up the lake. Bill was great, standing with his clipboard and stopwatch in hand, gently coaxing us into a sensible stroke pattern and away from our ergo mindset of thrashing a land based rowing machine.

As the muddy far bank loomed we encountered our first major problem – we couldn't steer. Then we saw the rudder floating on top of the water. It had detached itself from its mountings soon after our departure. We brought it aboard and back-steered with paddles. Hardly impressive to our audience freezing on the bank side. Still, we were happy, and rowing.

Lunch arrived with Buffy, Ali and Henry, who brought hot soup, quiche and crisps, devoured quickly in the bitter cold . By the end of the afternoon, we'd outgrown this stretch of water and needed something more challenging.

The following week we tackled Lake Windermere and our first bout of serious training. Rob had gone up on the Sunday evening and stayed in a B&B while I left in the small hours on Monday morning to avoid the traffic on the M5/6. We met in a lay-by at dawn and Rob gave me breakfast – one sausage and a piece of black pudding that he had managed to spirit out of his lavish Full Engish from the B&B. On the Fell Foote National Trust slipway at the southern most end of Windermere we spent an hour or so preparing the boat for launch. The first goal was to establish our double rowing positions with Rob on stroke and me in the bow seat. A very keen north-westerly gale force wind soon impressed on us the need to 'dig in' together and establish a steady rhythm. We found ourselves battling hard together against mounting waves for about 20 minutes without moving a metre. Rob kept on saying, "This is great!" I just grunted back "yeah mate" seriously wondering about his sanity. The rain maintained its horizontal attack on us as we slowly and surely got to grips with the elements and the boat. After four hours of serious rowing we eased into the calmer waters by Ambleside and tied up at the public jetty. We both felt pretty smug. The 15 miles or so of roughish water had left us feeling strong and ready for some more.

Before any more rowing we had to eat, and we had committed the cardinal sin of not eating for over nine hours. The human engine needs fuel to perform and although a day on Windermere without it was no big deal, out there on the Indian Ocean enough food would be critical to our success and survival. We hurried back to the boat and cooked a big 'all in' meal of beans, sausages and meatballs liberally laced with Coleman's mustard and Worcester sauce.

Goal number two was rowing at night. Into the murky gloom we set off rowing together for our first circuit, and despite the persistent drizzle we made good headway on a 4000 metre leg. The wind had died down with only occasional gusts. After another circuit we tied up and visited the pub for a pint, until the local singer and our consciences drove us back into the night.

Suitably warmed and refreshed we decided to hell with the islands, we were going to row back down south. Providing one of us was manning the spot light and we took it easy, we should be alright. Rob divided the route into legs of 10,000 metres.

About 15 minutes into my first leg, Rob said, "stop rowing, listen, what's that noise?" To me it sounded like a train coming down the lake; could the lake ferry still be running? Then in the spotlight we saw hundreds of Canadian geese desperately trying to take off as they fled from this intrusion on their sleep! We 'herded' them all the way down Windermere, as they repeatedly took off and landed in an effort avoid our tiny boat.

Sorry birds, it was a long night for all of us.

Then we took our boat to the sea....

It was five thirty in the morning on a freezing December day. An icy wind blew steadily out of the north, and a thick blanket of dark cloud all but extinguished the feeble first light of dawn. We had permission from the Army Sailing Association Club to use their private slipway running down into the Solent near Netley. But the concrete slipway was heavily iced, and the waters looked dark and unwelcoming.

Rob was waiting for me, wearing a vast green down coat. He was swearing under his breath about something. Nothing new. He was always swearing under his breath about something. I wasn't happy with the slipway ice and tried to find a shovel around the side of the rather dilapidated boathouse. While I was doing this Rob roared off in his car to try and find a café. He returned 20 minutes later. More cursing, no coffee. It was about then I realised that I'd forgotten both the kettle and the saucepan that we needed to brew up a hot lunch. I put off telling Rob. Maybe we'd find a kettle bobbing along in the Solent. Maybe Rob would have conquered his addiction to coffee by lunchtime.

With the Shogun sliding on the ice down the slipway we finally launched TRANSVenture into sea water. The pair of us walked into the muddy ice-cold water and clambered aboard. We were ready for lesson number one on the sea.

Southampton Sound leading to the Solent is the boating world's equivalent of the M25; there are ferries, boats and yachts of all shapes and sizes, and most of them seemed determined to get close to us. A very keen easterly wind was trying to drive us towards Southampton docks as we struck off together towards the Solent keeping close to the main water buoys. Water with a moderate swell was excellent for us as it revealed how difficult it was to row with any sort of rhythm when the waves came side-on to the boat. We practised turning into and away from the waves to see how the boat would react. She just rode over them as if to say "what's the big deal boys, you ain't seen nothing yet". It was encouraging to know that the boat was very buoyant. With the stern turned into the waves we found you could get a bit of surf on and travel some distance without much rowing. So we figured that as long as the waves on the Indian Ocean were always behind us, we would have no problems at all…

The other thing that helped was Rob's 'spurt power'. I was always safe in the knowledge that if we needed an extra 'spurt' over a few metres, Rob's power would deliver. He was definitely the guy you wanted with you in a tiny boat on the Indian Ocean.

We carried on past the Hamble inlet and into deeper water. We didn't realize how fast the tide was carrying us until we stopped close to a large metal buoy marking the deep water channel. One minute later and we were at least 200 metres away from it and 200 metres closer to the ferry lane. A good 30 minutes of double rowing put us back where we wanted to be. We decided to row up to Southampton docks and cook on the way. It was at this point that I broke the news to Rob about the saucepan. His face told me exactly how he felt. But I still managed to cook him a chilli con carne in its own can which he washed down with an isotonic sport drink. My attempt at cooking ravioli in its own can produced a burnt, filthy tasting meal, so I made do with an energy bar and a can of coke.

Low tide was at 3.00pm and knowing there were mud banks everywhere, we decided to get back while we could. Missing the tide would mean tying up to a buoy somewhere in deep water until 9.00pm and neither of us fancied that.

We had rowed for about four hours and felt perfectly fine. It was encouraging for our next trip to the Isle of Wight. I called my ex army mate,

Stuart McKean for some advice. As he lived in Lymington it seemed as good a start place as anywhere to have a bash around the Channel.

Early days in our boat training programme on the Solent between Southampton and the Isle of Wight.

We met up at the public slipway on a very cold morning. Reassuringly, the RNLI station was right beside the jetty. Less reassuring was the lack of other vessels on the water. Did they know something we didn't? Admittedly, a very stiff northerly wind was blowing at around force 6 to 7 and icicles hung off many of the yachts moored in the harbour. Still undeterred, we set off with Stuart's rib leading the way out into the channel.

We soon felt the swell building the further we got out. For the first time we understood the difference between 'neaps' and 'spring' tides as we battled gamely against stiff wind and tide. We'd told Stuart that we should be able to maintain a steady 6 knots with both of us rowing, but I was horrified to see on the GPS that we were struggling to get up to 1.5 knots. We dug in hard and upped the row rate. Four hours later we were sweating despite the arctic conditions and had only done around five nautical miles.

By now there were plenty of other vessels to distract us. The enormous RNLI boat was churning up and down with spectacular waves crashing off its bow as it went through its practise drills. We did our best to avoid the lanes of traffic coming in and out of Southampton and Portsmouth. Seeing the build-up of military vessels from the naval base in Portsmouth reminded us of the possible impending conflict out in the Middle East. As former soldiers we couldn't help pondering on the uncertain future for British forces as we struggled along in our tiny craft.

By 1500 hrs with Cowes just in sight it was obvious that we were not going to make Bembridge before last light and Stuart said that with worsening conditions it might be prudent for us to put in for the night. He towed us the last mile or so from the Prince Consort buoy into Cowes Yacht Haven marina where we tied the boat up for the night and caught a taxi to Bembridge and Rob's sister's holiday house. There, we heard the great news that Cathay Pacific could get the boat and ourselves out to Australia for a massive discount.

The following morning conditions had got sharply worse with a much stronger wind shifting to the North East. We decided to make it an 'admin' day and sort out the boat. As we gazed at the weather forecasts in the marina office I noticed there were three reports – for the west channel, middle channel and east channel. Feeling a little sheepish I asked which forecast applied to us Cowes. The staff looked at me strangely, and I immediately felt like an amateur for asking the question. It turned out that it was they who didn't know and were ***embarrassed.***

After lunch, we cast off in what was now a very choppy marina. Without steering we knew that we had one turn to make to get around the jetty into our preferred sheltered mooring. But the elements were against us and we were suddenly pushed towards the main jetty with no way of braking or turning safely without bashing into another boat. We were being forced towards the concrete pillar supports and potential disaster. Rob managed to get a leg out to fend the boat off the side of the jetty as my oars were slowly crushed against the pillar. How we got out of that I don't know as very quickly our next threat loomed – a walkway that just cleared the waterline with probably about three feet of daylight showing. "Duck!" I shouted just in time as we whistled through by the narrowest of margins – landing on a jetty belonging to the Royal Corinthian Yacht Club. It was quite incredible that we had escaped massive damage to our boat and ourselves, By then, all we could do was sit there laughing helplessly.

But the fun wasn't over yet. As we sat munching hot sausages and beans, and reflecting on our crazy route across the marina, there was a loud hissing sound from the cabin. One of the lifejackets had self-inflated in disgust. As Rob went down below to retrieve it, he put his full 15 stone onto a plastic hatch and shattered it. It was time to get away from the boat before we did something really stupid like sinking it, and we retired hurt to the local hotel for bath, supper and bed.

On the second day, conditions were much the same and we were forced to hug the shore for protection from the wind. We were glad to have Stuart on hand to guide us and tow us into Lymington. Despite (or perhaps because of) the 'incidents', we had learnt a great deal and felt we'd progressed well with our preparations.

We decided to ignore most of Stuart's parting advice: "Don't give up the day jobs lads. Forget about rowing across the Indian Ocean. But if you must, make sure you have a good life raft."

We didn't expect the weather to force us to spend so many **hours in our** tiny cabin. Had we known, we would have done more in the UK **to pad** her out, although we could do nothing about the hard metal edges **of our** vital equipment monitors. At first Rob and I made strenuous efforts **not to bump** into each other when lying down. But, as time passed and we **got more tired,** we unconsciously knocked into each other on every roll.

✯

DAY 9 – Monday 28th April
Location: 23:24:131S, 110:37:775E distance covered: 232nm

Alarmingly, during the night, several waves smashed into the side of the boat. They sounded like express trains. We became experts at anticipating the big ones and grabbing the sides of the coffin. At dawn I called Lee, who told me that his weather models showed the swell had increased to 7.1 metres during the night.

"We don't need your models, we're in the thick of it," I snapped irritably before quickly apologising. But Lee had more bad news. We were no longer on the fringes of the storm; the main force was travelling towards us.

Rob and I drew comfort from the fact that at least TRANSVenture was handling its battering well. We decided to make a hot drink. Inside the juddering, rolling cabin Rob precariously filled the kettle with some of our precious salinated water - just enough for two cups of coffee. It was entertaining to watch him light the gas ring - he kept burning his tee shirt. I kept the hatch open for fresh air and played a game of chicken with myself by peering out with one eye, ready to snap the hatch shut if a wave crashed onto the deck. My other eye tracked the gas flame roaring inches away from my face. After many spills and more burns, Rob decided that lukewarm water would do and we had our first heated drink in 36 hours. It tasted like nectar.

The winds dropped to 20 knots and the sun winked through the cloud cover. But the waves and swell were still too high to row safely and we kept busy with other tasks. I crawled on deck to haul in the second anchor and strap down the rollout solar panel, hoping that the weak sun would give us more power, especially for the watermaker, which we hadn't been able to use for two days. I washed my shorts and t-shirt in a bucket of seawater; they reeked from days of sweating in the coffin. Then I lay in the cabin reading while Rob played with the radio. We longed for good weather. I wondered what our families and friends thought of our slow progress. I read an email that Nick, my buddy in the UK, had sent to Buffy, joking that we must have landed on an island with lots of scantily clad women. What a thought, at that moment…

"Hey Buffy, I expect you have seen the progress or lack of progress on the boys' website. What are they playing at? Here we are expecting great things having seen them train like Olympic weight lifters, eat like horses and talk a big game and what are they doing, 30 miles a day?! If you ask me they have found a small previously unknown island, occupied by Amazonian scantily clad women, and have their feet up drinking coconut punch! Seriously though, it's a worry to hear they are going through the crappy weather, I hope their luck changes…"

★

DAY 10 – Tuesday 29th April
Location: 23:19:700S, 110:12:000E distance covered: 259nm

It was another rough night but I managed to sleep quite well despite falling on top of Rob several times. We decided to confront the swell and start rowing early. First, we had to pull in the sea anchor. This was not easy although at least my upper body muscles got a workout. We had agreed our tactics before setting sail. Rob rowed while I hauled. I hung over the front of the boat with our long gaff, snared the rope and then started a game of tug-o-war. I soon learnt to wear gloves for this operation. Meanwhile Rob rowed like mad to keep us facing the waves and move closer to the anchor. The most dangerous moment was as the parachute came on board. Countless times, Rob had to use the rudder and his strong arms to turn the boat quickly and prevent any side-on wave hits. In calm weather it was easy but in this swell it was a risky game.

Then the wind dropped and, for the first time in days, Rob and I could stand up on deck and strip off for a good wash. A quick check of our bodies revealed blistered fingers and hands (to be expected), sore backsides from all of the sitting and lying down, pressure sores from sliding inside the cabin, bruises on our hips and elbows and salt sores under our arms and backsides. On with the antiseptic cream and Vaseline. We reverted to rowing in two-hour shifts. We were determined to stay westwards, which meant rowing into the swell. Rick called to say that that the worst of the weather had now passed ... for another four days until Sunday. We had cleared the continental shelf but storms were coming from the Great Australian Bight and from the South.

"It's most unusual weather for this time of the year" he assured us. No kidding.

I was angry with our forecasters. "I've no idea why we pay so-called experts to get it so wrong," I told Rob.

Had we known what was to hit us within 24 hours of leaving Carnarvon we would have delayed our departure. Better to start a week or two later than blunder into unexpected, fearsome storms that wrecked our schedule and worried our families.

Experts such as Tony Bullimore and Robin Knox Johnson had advised us that a weather router was invaluable and so we had hired Lee Bruce, an American with a world reputation for his expertise. Then in Carnarvon we met Rick Friswell who worked for the Australia Metrological Office and offered free advice. It seemed to make sense to listen to both of them: Rick knew the coastline and local weather patterns while Lee worked with models and his brain. But I soon noticed that they seldom agreed…

It turned out that they were right for about 60 per cent of the time. I think they were wrong at the start for two reasons. First, and symptomatic of global warming, the weather was unusually volatile. Central Australia was going through its worst drought in living memory and a very late cyclone hit the coast to our North. Second, we were under pressure to set off, with the media constantly asking, "When are you going?" After one abortive launch, I suspect the forecasters convinced themselves that it would be all right for us to set off.

★

DAY 11 – Wednesday 30th April
Location: 23:14:303S, 109:47:500E distance covered: 284nm

More bad weather. The highlight of the day was speaking to Buffy and the children. Harry was very critical of our lack of progress and I agreed with him, although we had just crossed the 110 longitude, which was heartening.

Then Rob called me to come and see an unusual fish. As I pulled myself on deck it rolled under the bow in a flash of dark purple and turquoise. I lurched forward for a better look, jolted my shoulder against the gunwale and my sunglasses flew into the sea. The fish dived and the glasses followed.

Damn! I had a spare pair, but only one. We were just 280 miles into a 3,500-mile journey. I pondered on how alone we were and how dependent on our limited resources. What if the watermaker broke? Or if the solar panels stopped working? Or we lost our satellite access? Or - God help us - something rammed our hull? We were utterly reliant on our equipment. If it failed we might die. I hung over the edge, peering after my glasses and hoping that they might miraculously re-surface.

All afternoon we rowed. The salt cracks in my armpits widened and began to weep. Oh well, only another 3,250 miles to go.

In the evening the waves swelled and it was hard to row in the turbulence. The oars would grip the water and then suddenly lose all contact. It was a challenge keeping the bow of the boat facing into the waves – if we didn't, they hit us sideways, drenching us. They bounced Rob off his seat three times in twenty minutes and his habitual under-the-breath swearing became clearly audible. It was, he announced to the ocean, "a cake and arse party".

On our port side a huge flock of skuas feasted noisily on a carcass. It was too dark to see what they were eating but the sound was eerie.

I helped Rob put out the anchor for the night. Back in the coffin we tried to boost our spirits by listening to Dire Straits thrash their stuff at a gig eight thousand miles and a couple of light years away. But the band was no match for the raging elements. The boat's hull acted like an echo chamber for thunderous waves and we were enveloped in a discordant hubbub of the ocean, wind and rain.

✯

DAY 12 – Thursday 1st May
Location: 23:12:211S, 109:25:400E distance covered: 337nm

I woke with a start. My watch said 0630 hrs, so I'd been asleep since two. Panic gripped me: had I fallen asleep on watch duty? I shouted towards the hatch window, "Rob, is that you?" Then I laughed aloud. Who the hell else could it be? I lifted the hatch to see Rob wearing his mini disc player, rowing happily. I expected a good old bollocking but instead he calmly said, "Brew with you in 5 minutes; get the fags going".

I crawled out and rolled him a cigarette. It turned out that he hadn't bothered to wake me at 4 am. Like me he was anxious at our lack of pace and he couldn't sleep. We breakfasted at 0700 hrs and set off again. We wondered how long this caper would last. At least we were in it together. Our goal of finishing in 64 days or less had become an impossible dream. We knew we could average 50 or more nautical miles in days of good weather but we needed to be able to row around the clock. We'd had just one undisturbed period of 24 hours rowing. We got constantly soaked on deck, smashed about by the pitching and rolling and occasionally thrown painfully off the rowing seat.

Even having a crap was dodgy. We felt like the owners of the most dangerous toilet in the world. The routine was to 'bucket and chuck it'. You crawled to the bow end of the boat with baby wipes and the blue bucket. It was important not to confuse this with the yellow bucket – which was for washing up. Then you had to lower your shorts, gripping the bucket with one hand and the handrail with the other. Mother Nature took its course and, after carefully wiping the baby's bottom - using your ration of one sheet of baby wipes – you stood up and threw the contents into the sea … hoping to avoid the wind.

As I rowed, or tried to rest, I missed the bustle of our farm back home and thought constantly about my family. It distracted me from my worries about the vast distance ahead and the little behind. By now, the wind was blowing in our favour, which lifted our spirits. Rob's oar gate needed dousing with grease: we had not appreciated how quickly salt water clogged up everything and this became a daily chore.   We took turns rowing through the night in choppy conditions. Rob looked crazed when I relieved him, his eyes illuminated by a green glow from the GPS and his face manically contorted as he focussed on holding the line. Concentration was vital. I discovered that the boat became unstable if we strayed by just one degree from the GPS-set course. By dawn we had completed 53 nautical miles – our best 24 hours yet.

✭

DAY 13 – Friday 2nd May
Location: 23:14:698S, 108:37:967E distance covered: 379nm

We stopped rowing for breakfast and Rob did a telephone radio interview with Radio 8 Australia.

My left shoulder hurt so I got Rob to rub in aloe vera gel and I took some of Buffy's magical Bach Flower drops. The pain eased a little but I was unhappy with any injury at this stage in the journey. By lunchtime there was virtually no wind and, for the first time, we heard the ominous sound of water sloshing around in the hull ballast compartments. We took an hour to get it all out and re-apply mastic sealant around the cover, hoping that would be the end of it. From 1300 hrs it became very hot – my small deck thermometer showed 42 degrees. We were making about 2 knots an hour, which wasn't bad.

There was a beautiful sunset that night, and we felt privileged as we drank in the vivid shades of orange, red and gold. It helped that we were hundreds of miles from the nearest streetlight. I reflected on how tiny we were on this vast planet, as all around us, fish leaped up and plopped back into the sea. It was wonderful to sit on deck, eat our supper, forget about the weather and enjoy the best light show on earth.

*

CHAPTER THREE
HARD WORK

*

"It does not matter how slowly you go, so long as you do not stop"
Confucius

DAY 14 – Saturday 3rd May
Location: 23:21:533S, 107:52:414E distance covered: 411nm

Daylight revealed an unusually calm ocean with scarcely a ripple in the vast 360-degree panorama. This was a mixed blessing - almost a curse - since there was little or no wind to propel us. It needed hard graft. Lee Bruce praised our success in maintaining a westerly direction despite the northerly winds. He would try and track an easier route for us.

Rob examined our watermaker.

"Is it my imagination or is this thing making an odd noise?"

I agreed that the usual pulsing had turned to a stuttering beat. "Turn it off Rob, let's give it a rest," I said.

The watermaker was vital to the journey and I didn't dare think about it breaking down. It had probably sucked in some air during the storms and needed its valve bled. I would look at it later.

It was a fiercely hot, clear and still day. We wore sarongs to give our lower regions some air. These were much more comfortable to row in than shorts but thank goodness we didn't have a web cam on board!

I prepared to go overboard to look at the rudder, which had also been making strange noises. Rob was adamant that this was my job. Apparently his mother had warned him to stay away from the water. However, I'd be fine because he would stand guard with his precious shotgun in case of unwelcome visitors. I donned the face mask, tied on the safety rope and eased into the Indian Ocean. Perhaps if I went in quietly, nothing would see me! The water was delightfully cool and I briefly swam beside the boat, enjoying the respite before dipping my head into the abyss. The colours were amazing, turquoise green at the surface, and fading into blue, then the black of the deep. It was entrancingly clear but I could see and hear nothing - no fish, no sound, nothing. Submerging, I noticed a small build-up of scum along the hull - was it the start of a marine eco system making its home on TRANSVenture? It would have to be removed but that could wait till another day. I swam to the stern and noticed marks where the anti-foul paint had rubbed off. The marine plywood at the base of the rudder was chipped. A horrible thought crystallised. Fish bite marks, and by the look of it, something big. I quickly swam round to pull myself back on board.

Rob was unperturbed, saying that his gun would keep us safe.

"Look, I bought that gun specifically to see off any threat – I also bought it to shoot you if you became a pain in the arse. The man in the shop said that the weight of shot was big enough to bring down a flying goose at 100 feet, so a shark at 10 feet shouldn't be a problem."

I was unimpressed. "Mate, you're delusionary. A flying goose yes. All you'd do to a half ton angry shark at close range is make its eyes water. Anyhow, you were in the Gurkhas and it's well known you buggers couldn't hit a barn door even if it was staring you in the face. Put it away."

I thought about the damage a shark could do to our rudder (there was no spare). I quickly decided not to dwell on this and got back to rowing.

The temperature gauge showed 45 degrees on deck – our hottest day yet. Rowing or not, we both oozed sweat despite drinking copious amounts of water. I could row for no more than 15 minutes before having to take a break to gulp down a litre of fluid. We were getting through almost 8 litres in each two-hour rowing session.

A large turtle joined us. It was a beautiful green and about three feet in diameter. I stopped rowing to watch it effortlessly keep pace with us. There was me, grunting and groaning, pulling on a pair of three metre oars, while this animal coped easily with one-foot flippers. It stared at me beadily, as if to say, "What the hell are you doing out here?"

I asked it to clean the barnacles on the hull and, indignantly, it disappeared into the depths. Maybe it was the turtle and not a shark that had damaged to the rudder. It was a calming thought.

Wild Waters in the Roar

We had a gruelling night's rowing offset by the display of dazzling stars above. At one point, desperately tired, I saw my mother's smiling face looking down on me – was I going mad? The last 30 minutes of each stage were the worst and once I dozed off.

It was fun watching Rob come out on deck in the middle of the night. He usually started with an expletive as he hit his head and back on the cabin hatch and, for the next 15 minutes, I heard "Bugger this" and "Bugger that" as he trapped his sarong in the rowing tracks or got drenched by a 'sidewinder' wave.

I settled in the sweatbox and listened to important news on the World Service. Manchester United were eight points clear at the top of the table with a couple of games to go.

Then I heard Rob shouting excitedly.

"Cato, are you awake?"

He insisted on calling me Cato after the character in the Peter Sellers films.

"I am now. What is it?"

"Switch the radar reflector on pronto, I think we have a ship coming up on our stern"

"Bloody hell, wait a mo…No, there's nothing to report. What can you see out there?"

"Mate, I'm not being funny but it's a red light coming towards us. Strange thing is, it's not on the sea, it's in the air!"

"Don't worry, it's probably a plane going to Europe from Aus. Imagine that hey, stewardesses, drinks, comfy seats, normal toilets. What a thought…"

"Shit Cato. It's really close now and it's hovering. It's aliens I tell you. Get out here and see for yourself!"

I stumbled out to see Mars rising behind us in splendid, blood red glory.

Rob's first view of it would have been a dull and indistinct glow on the horizon but within minutes it was looming above us. I realised then how tired we both were but I never lost an opportunity to pull Rob's leg about the alien invasion.

Each morning the boat dripped with dew, inside and outside the cabin. Temperatures soared during the day and plummeted at night. I tried to sleep wearing all my clothes - tee shirts, Norwegian fleece, long trousers, foreign legion hat and rowing gloves. But, even swaddled up, I was chilled to the bone.

Mike Noel-Smith

★

DAY 15 – Sunday 4th May
Location: 23:24:170S, 107:19:999E distance covered: 438nm

After two weeks at sea I made some calculations. We had rowed 400 nautical miles with 2,800 to go. To reach Reunion Island within 50 days we had to cover 56 nautical miles a day compared with our actual average of 35 nautical miles. But I was convinced that we could speed up, with the right conditions and the wind behind us. We remained optimistic, fit and well, apart from minor complaints. Despite the heat and humidity we averaged around 2.5 knots that day. Rob appeared for his stag with a handkerchief around his head and his shotgun, just in case pirates appeared out of the mist. We did some 'burst' rowing at the end of each stage when we would both let rip for about 10 minutes. At one stage we had TRANSVenture up to 5.5 knots, an excellent speed.

My body ached now even during my rest time and the daytime temperature hit a record 46 degrees at half past two.

Everything was damp inside the cabin and I set up a clothesline running from the navigation mast to the rear cabin. The boat looked like a Chinese laundry.

I was also worried about the effect of the damp on our laptop. It had struggled to boot up a couple of times and was our only means of communication for emails and downloading weather data.

At 1800 hours BBC Radio 5 Live called for a chat and I imagined some of my mates driving along wet, dismal English motorways and smiling as they heard about two nutters on the Indian Ocean.

Radio 5: Well hi Mike and Rob, how are you? Some of our listeners will find it interesting to hear that you are rowing from Australia to Africa. Are you mad?

Mike: Good morning to you I believe and hello from a sun-setting Indian Ocean. We are fine thank you and going along as we speak at 2.5 knots with Rob rowing and me inside the cabin that we call our coffin. Mad no – just two blokes out for a row, they do it all the time on the Thames!

Radio: That sounds great, back here we have been watching you progress – how are you doing on your way to Africa?

Mike: We have had some tough days and some good ones. To be honest if we can achieve 40-50 miles in a day then we are very happy. The problem is that Mother Nature doesn't always oblige and we end up dealing with winds on the nose which definitely slows us down. That said we are happy with our line (direction) and all in all things are good.

Radio 5: How long will it take you?

Mike: Around 90 days in total. We originally hoped for around 64 days, but frankly that's wildly optimistic given the conditions.

Radio 5: Talking of which, can you describe the sea conditions?

Mike: Right now it's as calm as a sleeping baby – hardly any wind to speak of and swell which is rolling into us gently. On the other hand, we have had the mother and father of conditions when the winds howl so much you cannot hear yourself speak let alone be understood. The waves and swell start to build into watery tower blocks that pound against the boat and you can't see anything through the spray unless you put on goggles. When it's really having a go, it's very impressive but also extremely frightening.

Radio 5: Well you guys take care and row hard. We will talk again when you are closer to Africa. Any message you want to send out to anyone this morning on their way to work?

Mike: My office is the beauty of the ocean, what's yours? Say no more!

We ate supper quietly, gazing at the millpond that was the ocean. All around, fish were jumping, dodging the predators that roamed in the dark. Then dark clouds formed to our south and the sea started kicking out in all directions. I had never seen such a rapid transformation. We were being driven backwards. Rob was trying to adjust his oar gate when a violent 'side winder' wave rudely tipped him out of the boat. Before I could do anything he had hauled himself back at a remarkable speed although he cut his arm slightly, leaving blood in the water for any probing sharks. This episode taught us to wear safety harnesses whenever the sea rose above a gentle swell. Rob gamely kept rowing until the waves crashed over the top of the boat and there was no option but to deploy the sea anchor and batten down the hatches.

⋆

DAY 16 – May Bank Holiday Monday 5th May
Location: 23:24:170S, 107:19:999E distance covered: 452nm

The World Service announced that Manchester United had won the title – good news for Rob's father who was a keen supporter. Rob went through the challenge of making breakfast in the storm – good man - while I lay thinking about our schedule. We might take another 80 days, which would mean finishing in late July. We just needed the wind to shift to our advantage. As always, I felt sure this would happen.

I spoke to Buffy on the satellite telephone and she told me that they had sold Ana, my MG sports car, for £4,000. There was no point moaning since Buffy needed the money and I had no need for Ana on the ocean. With school fees due it was the only asset that we could quickly liquidate. I felt guilty about leaving the family behind to fend for itself.

Everyone who emailed us seemed impressed by our straight line across the map.

I just wished we could go faster. At least our weathermen were predictable. First Rick called to say that Tuesday and Wednesday would be all right, but conditions would deteriorate again by the weekend. Then Lee told me that rowing would be hard for the next few days before it got easier.

It was another dreadful night as we involuntarily battered each other with elbows, knees and feet. By 0500 hours I could stand it no more and I crawled out to make an early breakfast of cold cereal and lukewarm tea.

✯

DAY 17 – Tuesday 6th May
Location: 23:55:628S, 106:59:200E distance covered: 502nm

I realised that it would be difficult to go westwards as the swell was still trying to drive us north. But, by late afternoon, the wind changed and lent us a hand. It remained choppy but we were determined to cover a good distance. As I rowed, daydreaming, the ominous outline of a large, dark fin grabbed my attention. At first the black triangle was about 50 metres away. Then it disappeared, only to re-appear 20 metres from the boat, with another fin just

Wild Waters in the Roar

behind. My heart thumped and I called Rob out from the cabin. Our two oceanic white tip sharks were back. Were they stalking us? I remembered a passage from Jim Shekhdar's book about shark attacks out in the Pacific Ocean. Those beasts followed him for days on end. He waged war on them and for a solo rower it must have been terrifying. At least I had Rob and his gun with me. It was unnerving whenever the sharks disappeared. Where were they? Were they about to attack? I stopped rowing because I thought it might antagonise them. After half an hour, I got bored and started rowing again. "Come on you bastards, if you want to have a go then get on with it", I shouted.

Thankfully they did nothing but keep pace with us for a few more hours.

Coming off my stag I lit up a fag and gave one to Rob. It looked like we would run out of my supplies of baccy within three weeks. I convinced myself that Rob must have a secret stash somewhere.

I thought about how strong I felt, despite aching muscles that needed stretching at the end of each stag. Our trainer back home had predicted that we would peak about a month into the journey.

We had trained intensively because we knew it was going be tough. How did you get fit enough to row 3500 nautical miles across an ocean where the sea temperature seldom dipped below 28 degrees and the air temperature could exceed 40 degrees? How many times would the oars dip into the sea - 20,000, 200,000, 2 million? How hard was it to propel a 21-foot rowing boat weighing almost a ton? What strain would that put on muscle groups over 70 or more days? I didn't doubt that the physical effort would be huge, but what about our psychological and emotional state? When you added sleep and food deprivation, it seemed like a nightmare. We were entering new terrain – this type of extreme endurance would require specialist help.

I was worried about was my age. Rob was just 30 and, at six foot two and around 15 stone, he could hold his own with just about any gym programme. But could I say the same at 45? At Rob's age, I was climbing big mountains in Europe and Central America. I set myself high standards in the army and tried to maintain them whatever the situation demanded. I relished the challenge of taking my body to its limits and even ran a marathon with no training. Fifteen years on though, I was beset by doubts. This was not like Saturday morning rugby coaching, playing in the odd veterans' game or a run with the dogs. This was hard-core. Could I make the grade? I knew one thing: I wouldn't go if I could not get fit enough. That would be reckless, and unfair on Rob. What's more, my pride was at stake, and I'm a bad loser.

Rob and I agreed not cut any corners. Enter Mr. Bill Black, coach to the elite athletes.

I told Bill of our plans at an event in Ireland in July, when Rob and I were ready to quit our jobs and concentrate full time on the expedition. I was taken aback by his initial reaction. He seemed shocked, muttering, "Oh dear, oh dear, so much to do" and "Are you two mad?"

The next morning at breakfast he was more forthright.

"You bastards, I haven't slept a wink all night. You don't know how much we have got to do!"

We gladly became his 'gladiators'.

We started in earnest at a new Holmes Place fitness suite in Fulham. Typically Rob managed to blarney himself free membership while he trained for the row. I was new to this 'yuppy' gym scene. Everyone seemed driven by appearance.

But we were used to arduous physical challenges. We had both served in the infantry, which meant being able to march many miles with heavy packs of up to 50kg, dig six-foot trenches and fight hand-to-hand with the enemy if necessary. Rob even played rugby professionally for Ulster, London Irish and Newbury until, like me, he suffered a serious injury. We knew about pain and suffering but we still had to steel ourselves for a ruthless training routine – in the gym and later on in the water – lasting nearly eight months.

Bill was our coach and inspiration. He gave us targets and monitored our progress faithfully. He made us keep daily diaries recording what we had eaten, what exercise we had done and how we were feeling. Maintaining good morale and mental strength is crucial to any athlete preparing for an event. I had some bad days but over time I could see that I was improving. It was a life lesson: set your goals but record milestones along the way to stay motivated, enthusiastic and focused.

I was very concerned about my back. After it was damaged playing rugby I had an operation to remove a ruptured disc and cracked vertebrae. A titanium block was inserted in the 'gap' and I wasn't entirely convinced by the surgeon's reassurance that I could do everything I wanted except bungee jumping. When I started training on the rowing machine, I felt excruciating pain and thought that my back would give out and I might damage myself for life. I prayed every night that it would get better. The pain didn't go away, but it didn't get worse. It was like a time bomb that never detonated. The press thought this was a hoot – a man with a broken back - who had never rowed before - was going to conquer an ocean. How British!

In September Bill arranged a visit to the British Olympic Medical Centre in Harrow where many elite athletes go for physical testing under laboratory conditions.

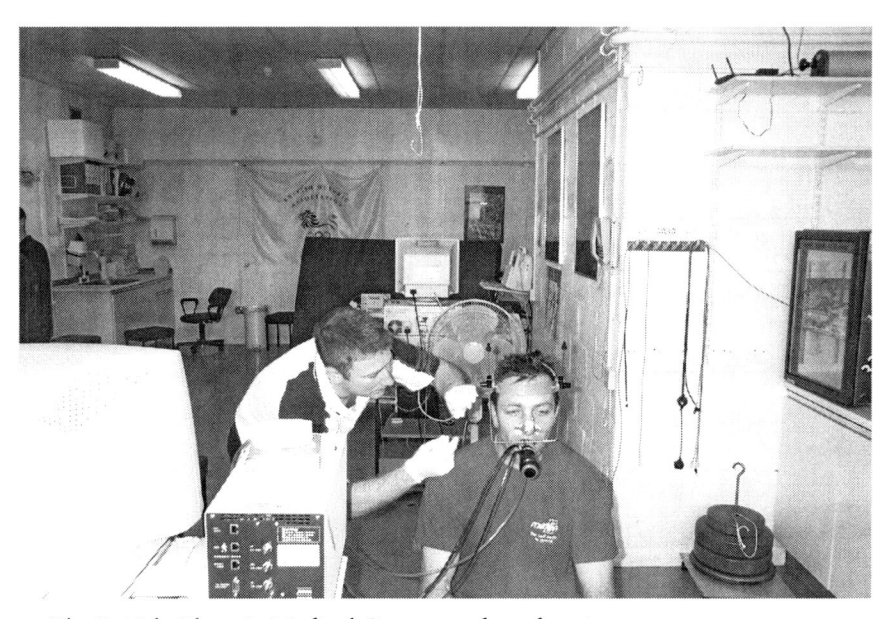

The British Olympic Medical Centre conducted various tests on us to see our capacity to endure physical pressure

VO2 Max testing measures your ability to use oxygen. The harder the exercise, the more oxygen your body needs. Eventually, however, your body reaches its limit for consuming oxygen, even if the exercise intensifies. This is known as maximal oxygen uptake and it indicates which athletes will do well in endurance races – although it can't predict who will win. For us it was all about hammering the ergo rower. This was a nasty business, with four-minute bursts interspersed with 30 second rests when blood samples were taken. We also went through a series of tests looking at our muscle expansion and core body balancing, oxygen intake, heart rate, height and weight. It was a bewildering day and I was worried that the staff would question my commitment because I had owned up to drinking and smoking.

45

The results put Rob ahead of me on all counts. I had expected this but I vowed to beat him in at least one discipline when we returned after Christmas. I am pleased to report that I did even better than that! The staff were full of praise for my improvement, boosting my morale tremendously.

Our appetites grew as our hyperactive bodies craved more fuel. It was inspiring after three months to discover that I had gained two stone in weight and become strikingly stronger and faster.

Running was my favourite exercise and I increased my daily distances to between five and eight miles. A couple of weeks before setting out for Australia I ran to Monmouth and back, a total of 29 miles non-stop.

Christmas Day, and I phoned Rob in Ireland to remind him that we had to train.

"Happy Christmas mate, how's it going?"

"Great, Cato and Happy Christmas to you too. We are just about to go to church and then getting stuck into champagne and turkey. What are you lot up to?"

"We've done the early church service and now its presents time. I'm leaving Buffy to get on with the turkey et al. I'm off for a run. Remember, we have a training session today – when are you doing yours?"

"Come on Cato. Today! I'm sure Bill won't mind us missing just one session?"

"Mate, no way – he would expect this of us. He's trained Olympic athletes for God sake – do you think Daly Thompson hung up his training shoes on Christmas Day? No he didn't; he wanted to make sure that nothing would stop him in his goal. Anyway, what's two hours in a day? Think of it, how many other ocean rowers are training today – I'll wager not one. But we are…"

"OK, ok I get the message – I'm on my bike as we speak!"

"Good man, and remember, only two glasses of booze and keep off the mince pies fat boy."

I had learned about Daley Thompson from Frank Dick, the former British Olympic Coach. Daley was determined to train every day, including Christmas and New Year's Day. He thought it was unlikely that any of his rivals would train on these days and he wanted to keep a mental and physical edge over them. We had no rivals but we knew that we had to make sacrifices to succeed. We had to row an ocean, and there would be many other Christmases to sit back amongst the wrapping paper, sherry and mince pies.

I set out on my seasonal run after the family present opening. It was particularly memorable because the local stream was in full spate. I misjudged its width and fell in…

"Come on!" Rob yelled triumphantly to the elements.

At almost midnight we at last we crossed the 500 nautical miles point.

Poking my head out into the dark I reminded Rob that we still had more than five times that distance to go. It was a sobering thought.

★

DAY 18 – Wednesday 7th May
Location: 23:02:789S, 106:01:671E distance covered: 557nm

Coming off at 0600 hrs I made up our energy drinks and dived into the cabin for the latest weather update. The forecast was not good. We could expect an overcast day with building seas and rain. It seemed that for every reasonable day we got two bad ones. I told Rob, who looked determined. We pulled out all the stops that day, not stopping even to cook lunch or supper. During my afternoon session it started to pour – our first rain since we left the UK on April Fools Day. We quickly stripped off and applied soap, taking grateful advantage of nature's shower. It was heavenly standing up on the deck relishing droplets as big as ping-pong balls. It was the best feeling I'd had since leaving dry land – at last I could wash the salt from all parts of my body. It's difficult to explain the exhilaration at this everyday function.

The rain torrented through the night. Neither of us had weatherproofs although they wouldn't have provided much protection. We rowed in turns to the sound of the seat grinding as it to-ed and fro-ed and the rain splattered the water everywhere. Occasionally a squall would resonate, like an orchestra building to a wild crescendo. Then the wind calmed a little and the rain's beat became more controlled and gentle.

It was no fun squeezing back into wet clothes at the beginning of each stage. The sheepskin covers on our rowing seats were like saturated squeegee mops.

Mike Noel-Smith

⭐

DAY 19 – Thursday 8th May
Location: 22:58:176S, 105:13:747E distance covered: 600nm

It was a grey morning with cold rain and no hint of sunlight. I passed my rowing time by attaching strange meanings to the cloud formations. On my port side I watched a huge skyborne elephant while on the starboard, sidecars jockeyed for position on an imaginary start line. Was I losing the plot? The wind pressed from the south at about 10 knots and the swell bobbed at 2 metres. These were relatively good rowing conditions.

I started up the water maker despite its unhealthy noise and the lack of sunshine. We needed to generate supplies as we had very little left in a couple of two-gallon containers strapped in the 'well'.

A shoal of Dorado fish swam close to the boat and provided our day's entertainment. They moved with rapier-like speed. Streaks of yellow and blue lightening flashed past under the boat, one after another. I estimated that they weighed 10 to 20 kilograms each. They were very powerful, acrobatic swimmers.

With no sharks in sight I grasped my chance to nab a tasty fish for supper. I love fishing and was poaching trout at the age of eight. A fellow fanatic called Geoff had given me my kit for this journey - spinners ranging from small ones up to large, four-inch lures meant to attract big game fish. All were brightly coloured and it was a pleasure just to open the box and look at them. But up till now, my high hopes had always been dashed. Whenever I felt a fish bite and started pulling, the line suddenly went slack. Then I'd find a remnant of fish head hanging grimly from the lure or else the lure and line had disappeared. I discovered that the fish were biting the lure and sharks were biting the fish – a terrible cycle. There were so many fish in the ocean but my only chance of landing one was if the sharks had a day off.

No sharks today, but as if by magic, when I returned with my kit, the Dorados had vanished. Rob gave me no end of a ribbing.

Rick called to warn us to expect torrential rain and big seas over the next 24 hours. Nothing new. We listened obsessively to our weather reports, hoping with every call to get better news.

DAY 20 – Friday 9th May
Location: 23:07:230S, 104:24:190E distance covered: 640nm

We made just 14 nautical miles that night in porridge-like conditions. We reckoned we were stuck in an eddy again. The ferocious rain forecast by Rick didn't materialize but we still endured a persistently heavy drizzle. I tied a bucket to the roof of the cabin to catch some rainwater but, whenever it got half full, the slightest sideways movement dumped the precious contents into the sea.

Radio 5 Live called us for another interview. They were either very interested in our journey, or they had nothing else worth reporting in the world.

During my first two-hour session of the day I managed 5.8 nautical miles, a personal best. We must have broken through the eddy system. If we could maintain speed we would make good headway.

The watermaker was gurgling so I bled the valve and filled the pre-chamber. It started making water again, albeit noisily.

The sea was running to the South East with winds of around 12-15 knots, which was excellent for us, and the swell remained at a very manageable 2.5 metres. Riding on the back of a decent swell we raced TRANSVenture up to 6.3 knots. It was terrific gliding at speed, accompanied by a swishing and whooshing as the boat was propelled through the water. In these conditions we didn't have to row. The boat suddenly accelerated forward as if a giant hand had grabbed the stern. I slipped the oars through their gates and onto the deck and quickly grabbed the rudder lines down at our feet. The knack was to surf along the top of the wave and not go down its centre. If I misjudged the manoeuvre there was a risk of digging the bow of TRANSVenture into the bottom of the wave, flipping the boat right over. It took some getting used to but, once mastered, it was a great game.

I handed over to Rob and crawled into the cabin and read our very first text message on the satellite telephone (I hadn't realised that we had this). It was from my 17-year-old son William and said, simply: "Make sure you continue to row your bollocks off!"

Rob broke into my paternal thoughts, shouting, "Not being funny mate, but this water maker sounds as sick as a parrot".

I went to switch it off. "We will leave it to cool down and then I'll start it up again. If I've got to take it apart, we will have to wait for a calm day".

Secretly, I was worried that a complete ring change was needed. Although I had done a day course in Southampton, I didn't feel confident about taking the watermaker to pieces. Making repairs in a warm classroom was one thing. Out here on the briny it was all down to me.

Buffy emailed to say that our local pub, The Black Swan, had raised more than £200 for our charity SPARKS on May Bank Holiday. This was encouraging news. God, I missed my family. Years before, when I was serving in the Army, it was usual for me to be away for months at a time and we easily muddled through the separations. My outlook had changed as I got older and I was surprised at how homesick I felt.

Rick told us that the wind would strengthen, as a system blew off the Great Australian Bight, bringing greater swells that could help us if we harnessed their power. During the night I became aware of amazing phosphorescence sparkling off the end of my oars as I dipped them into the water. As the waves broke over the deck they sprayed green and yellow bursts of colour, like tiny stars washing over the deck. It was a mesmeric sight.

★

DAY 21 – Saturday 10th May
Location: 23:25:283S, 103:49:763E distance covered: 704nm

It became too rough and we reluctantly deployed the anchor at 0300 hours. I stayed out for a while trying to video the starbursts while hanging onto the handrail. After ten minutes I realised that this was too dangerous. I could easily drop our only video camera into the sea and maybe join it. I felt vulnerable without the umbilical cord of my safety harness, which could not reach the deck jackstays where I stood. If I fell overboard, the boat would soon leave me behind, Rob would hear nothing and there was no way that I could swim hard enough to get back. I took sanctuary in the cabin, gripped by the thought of being alone in the dark, floating in the ocean with no prospect except death.

Lying down I could not escape from this image of doom. I wondered what it was like to drown. Would it be painful or just like drifting to sleep? Would my body float or sink to the depths? How would Rob explain it to Buffy and the children? With these macabre thoughts I finally dozed off.

At 0700 hours we started rowing again. I crawled up to the bow to pull in the sea anchor. It turned out to be my toughest fight yet. While trying to grab the leading rope I lost my grip and dropped the gaff into the depths. What a stupid thing to do. I had forgotten to tie on the wrist strap to prevent exactly this from happening. For a split second I thought about diving in to get it. But it was gone and had another 3000 metres to fall before hitting the ocean bed. I was mortified. The gaff gave me crucial help in getting hold of the anchor rope.

"Don't worry - just nip out and buy another one!" shouted Rob.

I had to climb onto the bow end of the boat and lean right out to grasp the rope. After 15 minutes and a soaking from crashing waves I eventually succeeded and collapsed in a heap on the deck, surrounded by 80 metres of tangled rope. My shoulders, arms and chest had been pushed to the physical limit. Rob stayed very cool and pragmatic about it all. This was one of our core strengths as a team - an ability to accept difficulties and not blame each other. We had mutual respect and trust. Instead of seeing problems we looked for solutions. I would have plenty of time to think of one on my next rowing session.

I used the video camera again so that we had some coverage of bad weather. It was difficult with the boat rolling but I knew that we needed good footage if we were to make a documentary.

The winds wailed and again we steered with the rudder guide ropes while leaving the oars on deck. It required intense focus but we achieved eight knots at one point. It beat the hell out of rowing! It was an exhilarating if manic experience as the boat plunged into troughs and then burst dramatically on top of the swell. We struggled but we also enjoying the challenge of the ocean.

*

CHAPTER FOUR
MIND GAMES

*

"All men dream, but not equally. Those who dream by night in the dusty recesses of their mind awake in the day to find that it was vanity; but the dreamers of the day are dangerous men, for they may act upon their dreams with open eyes to make it possible"

T.E. Lawrence

DAY 22 – Sunday 11th May
Location: 23:18:403S, 102:51:691E distance covered: 745nm

Rob woke me at 0400 hrs.

"No, you've got it wrong, it's not my turn, bugger off".

Another bang on the cabin window and begrudgingly I crawled out on deck.

The ocean was calm and the stars were fading in the sky ready for the dawn. Rob gave me his usual briefing about the distance he had covered on his two-hour stag and the bearing I should stick to. He drained the last drops from his water bottle before disappearing into the cabin. There were a couple of loud 'buggers' as he banged his head on the side of the cabin, followed by silence.

I crawled onto my rowing seat, clipped on my harness and eased the oars through their gates and into the water. After a gulp of my orange-flavoured energy drink I made the first of many strokes, propelling TRANSVenture ever closer to our goal. Somewhere, over the curve of the planet, lay Reunion Island - a speck of volcanic rock nestling in a cornucopia of water. It was more than 2000 miles away. Exhausted as I was, I felt this tough trip still beat working.

After two hours and about 2500 strokes of the oars, I readily handed over to Rob. He had emptied the contents of one of the water containers from the well into his bottle and so I switched on the watermaker. It spluttered and made a dreadful noise akin to a grinder cutting deep into hard metal. I switched it off and it ground painfully to a halt. The bloody thing was knackered.

"Shit Rob, this is serious. As they said in Apollo 13 – " we have a problem."

"Can't you fix it?

"I will try but I don't like the sound. If it were just bad water coming through then it would be the O rings or a seal somewhere, but you heard the noise, it's metal grinding on metal. Something it off skew inside and that means trouble. I'll take it apart and have a look. That's a long job and just accept for the time being that it might be f*cked. If it is broken, it'll be a problem getting enough drinking water. Tell you what, let's not tell anyone until we know it's definitely knackered."

The watermaker was our main source of fresh water. Below deck we had 50 gallons of tepid water as ballast for the boat and an emergency drinking supply. It would probably give us drinking water for 10 days but we faced another 50 or so days at sea. I set about examining the infernal machine, opening up the deck locker where it was stored and unbolting it from the hull. The tubular beastie was about two foot long, with a perplex jar attached and pipes running in all directions. Weighing about 12 kgs, it was one of our heaviest pieces of equipment and arguably the most important. It worked by sucking in seawater and pressurising it through a membrane to purify it. It spat salt and minerals back into the sea while fresh water trickled into a container.

After much sucking and blowing I established that there were no blockages in the pipes. The problem appeared to be a lack of pressure in the pre-filter jar, which could only be resolved by laboriously opening the machine and replacing the 'O' rings -several rubber gaskets of varied sizes. I undid countless nuts and bolts and then opened the replacement pack, discovering to my horror that the largest and most important 'O' ring was missing. Desperately, I phoned the chandlers in Southampton for advice.

A receptionist told me their engineer was away but she'd get him to call me back. I gave her our satellite telephone number and our latitude and longitude. She was silent for a moment.

"So can't you bring it in for us to check then?"

Wild Waters in the Roar

Our source of fresh water was broken beyond repair with external damage and an internal gearbox seizure to the water maker

I guffawed and, with a cheery (in the circumstances) goodbye, left her to file her nails back in Blighty.

Rob was parched after four hours of non-stop rowing but remained as sanguine as ever.

"Don't worry mate, let's get another container out of the hold for the moment".

However the waterproofing mastic had bonded the entrance to the hold like superglue. After trying to ease around the seal with a knife I resorted to hammers, knives and, finally, an axe to bust open a hole just big enough to get out one container. Now we had a gash in the deck and I didn't know whether to laugh or to cry. We plugged the gap as best we could with spare marine ply board and plastic bags.

It looked like we would have to use our manual watermaker every day. We were in a deadly serious predicament. I recalled the instructor on our ocean survival course outlining the disturbing effects of water deprivation. In temperatures constantly over 100 degrees, you couldn't hope to survive without water for more than three days of escalating unpleasantness. Dehydration would strike quickly, quickly making you irrational. Your blood volume would drop, constricting the blood vessels and causing mounting headaches, muscle cramps and dizziness before you died. It was an uplifting lecture.

That evening we ploughed on despite heavy seas and high winds – we had to keep up the momentum to get another 50-mile day in. However, at 2300 hrs I was forced to stop. Water was pouring onto the deck as we slid across rather than with the swell. The scuppers could not drain the surface fast enough and it felt sitting in a bath. The bow of the boat plunged down the front of a wave and dug into the trough while, simultaneously, the weight of water from an incoming wave pushed up the stern. I really thought we might pitch pole and heard Rob smashing around inside the cabin as he was flung forward against the main hatch. I tied down everything on deck, dropped the sea anchor and crawled inside.

At 0300 hrs I got up for a wee. Outside it was watery pandemonium and I resigned myself to pissing all over the deck in uncontrollable squirts.

★

DAY 23 – Monday 12th May
Location: 23:13:080S, 102:25:877E distance covered: 764nm

The sea was fiendish – the worst yet. It seemed to be playing games with our minds. Could this ocean and its gods be trying to harm us? Long bands of waves rolled menacingly towards us, with the crest edges breaking into spindrift and well-defined streaks, following the path of the Force 7 or 8 wind.

We were noticeably lower in the water, probably because the hole in the deck invited the waves to fill the ballast area. This was destabilising the boat and so I strapped on my swimming goggles, tied on my harness and crawled up to try and plug the hole. But it was no good, I was being tossed around like a rag doll as water flooded the deck. Back in the cabin, we had our first emergency meeting.

"What do you reckon?" asked Rob.

"Looks like we are in the shit, to be honest." I said.

"We are very low in the water so we could easily turn upside down and I doubt if we'd self right. We'd best stop rowing for now".

Our eyes locked as the storm raged outside.

I broke the awkward silence.

"Right, what about calling Rick?"

"And exactly what good will that do, Einstein?"

Rob was right, of course. I was clutching at straws and could only see the worst scenario – TRANSVenture might sink.

But then Rob said: "You're right mate, we are in the shit".

It was the first time we'd had such a frank exchange and not tried to laugh it all off.

We prepared in case we had to abandon our drunkenly lurching boat. The prospect of getting into the life raft was bleak. We put our life jackets to hand and filled the grab bag with food, water, spare GPS, satellite phone with fully charged batteries, flares and VHF radio.

I called Buffy.

"Hi Bears." It was my nickname for her. I listened to the crackling static before hearing her reply from 9,000 miles away.

"Hello darling, you shouldn't be calling?"

My call was outside our agreed sequence.

"Sorry, but I really wanted to hear your voice as it's a bit shitty out here at the moment."

"What's the matter?"

"We are in the mother of all storms, and the constant battering is not good for morale!"

"I can hear it in your voice. Just calm down, everything will be ok."

"No, you don't understand, the sea is horrendous. We can't do anything other than hide in the coffin. I have to say I'm frightened the boat won't take this much longer."

"What are you trying to say? Are you sinking?" Now there was alarm in her voice.

"No, it's not that bad, I just thought you and the girls could get together and tell someone to switch the storm off."

I realised now that I had overstepped the mark and was frightening her.

"Sweetheart, just ask the universe and it will respond. Don't worry, everything will be fine."

"Ok, got to go now, take care. I'll call you tomorrow. Love you."

She knew me so well that I feared she'd guess that I'd wanted to talk to her in case it was the last time. Her gentle voice assuaged my panic but I felt guilty about sharing my fears.

We were pounded incessantly through the night. An unusually loud crash of waves was followed by a sickeningly slow rotation as the boat tipped over to the port side. Everything fell out of the side lockers and I ended up on top of Rob. The cabin light went off and I fumbled with my head torch to switch it on. I look at Rob. His eyes reflected my own cold terror.

I thought of my family and of how stupid it would be for me to drown out here. No one would find our bodies and that would be so cruel for them.

After about three minutes, the boat mercifully righted itself and for the next couple of hours we sat up, bracing ourselves for more aquatic acrobatics.

Lee called at dawn to reassure us that we should have calmer conditions in the next 18 hours. But he warned that another big nasty would be with us on Wednesday or Thursday. Wonderful news.

We weren't sure how the boat would withstand it all. Apart from the hole in the deck I was worried about the storm anchor. It seemed to be under a huge strain and we didn't want it to take a chunk of the boat with it.

The wind strength on Lee's model was 35 knots gusting to 45 knots. All – ha – we needed was good weather to end this nightmare. The watermaker saga seemed almost insignificant – we didn't know if we would need water for much longer.

★

DAY 24 – Tuesday 13th May
Location: 23:13:214S, 101:67:977E distance covered: 808nm

We looked out nervously at a dark grey mass of sea interspersed by the white flashes of breaking water on top of the building swell. TRANSVenture was bucking about like a wild horse at a rodeo. Anything not tied down inside the cabin was being thrown around. The howling wind sounded like a hurtling steam train and our wind indicator flag outside rattled manically.

I felt a growing sense of helplessness and panic as the waves relentlessly pounded.

Thoughts flooded my brain: 'you're not going to get out of this one', 'how do you like it now smartarse?', 'who's going to be there to pick up the pieces?' and 'not as brave as you thought you were hey?'

I screamed at the din, "Why don't you sod off you bastards?"

I was angry because it wasn't meant to be this way. We should have been enjoying the challenge, not terrified and cooped up in a floating coffin.

I looked at Rob and could see that he too was feeling the strain. It made me feel better knowing that I was not alone. Although we would not admit it, we were desperately tired, despondent and very frightened.

At times like this that I wondered if the sea gods were deliberately toying with us before sending us to our doom. I remembered the words of an ancient Aborigine who I had met in Carnarvon a few days before we set out:

"Be sure to thank the Wandjina of the big wet every day for keeping you safe."

I had been resting on a bench after gentle jog around the town and was joined by this elderly gentleman whose creased face resembled the gnarled trunk of an oak tree.

He asked me what I was doing, listened carefully and then told me that the ocean had many bad spirits but also good ones.

I thanked him for the tip and started my run back to the hotel. Did these guys really believe in spirits? Did I?

I knew nothing about this ancient civilisation, with one of the world's oldest surviving cultures. Next time I went to Australia I would learn more about their customs and myths and what they thought of life today.

The Aborigine's warning struck a chord with me now: the ocean indeed controlled our destiny. The weather could change in an instant. When it was calmer we sometimes saw rain curtains, lightening and choppy waves in the distance and we prayed that they didn't come our way.

I found in this storm that I was more open to Buffy's spiritualism. Before I set out I had mainly been pleased that her outlook was helping her to cope with my departure. But now I felt that meditating and positive thinking by Buffy and her friends might really help us.

I thought back to how, a couple of nights before the boat went to Heathrow, Buffy and her friends conducted a 'blessing' on TRANSVenture. They left behind various items from 'terra firma', which I hid in the forward cabin. These included feathers, rice and a beautiful hand-sculptured starfish that Ness had done for us. I was also given a large piece of amethyst that I was going to glue to the bow of TRANSVenture. I was determined to take these all these items across the ocean. The girls had great faith in TRANSVenture and her ability to carry two men safely across a vast stretch of water. Knowing their resolute faith gave me strength as well.

Buffy adds: "No preparation is whole without some form of ceremony. The act of ceremony adds energy and intent to the outcome. Be it Johnny Wilkinson before his kick, a priest before communion, or the naming of a ship before her maiden voyage, ceremony is an acknowledgment to the spirit of the venture/act.

"With the intention to bless TRANSVenture, the process had already begun in the ether. One of my group was studying Shamanism and asked if she could create the guiding for the ceremony. She wrote "the art of ritual is a medium that offers us a language of patterns, imagery and belonging, giving us the sense of security we need to take the risks and make the changes. It is a pause in time, a break from the tumbling swirls and eddies of life's river. It gives an opportunity to check our beliefs, both those that are sound and those that need to be changed. It reveals the world as sacred, guiding us to relate more closely to its creativity and its essence, to understand more respectfully the spirit of nature, its power and potential.

"After offerings and many inspirational words asking for the spirits of nature to guide and keep safe the boat, our ceremony ended with a prayer that I had written for the occasion.

"A Blessing for TRANSVenture
May the Rob Abernethy and Noel-Smith venture bring love,
peace and understanding to all those touch by their actions,
May this vessel be their perfect home, for harmony and nourishment of
heart, body and soul during their voyage of enlightenment,
May the divine light shine within them and upon them,
carrying them safely to their destination,
With thanks I give love, light and blessings to all involved past,
resent and future,
Thank you for showing us the light and being with us today
Peace be with you
So may it be!"

Wild Waters in the Roar

We were ravenous and Rob busied himself cooking a lukewarm mince casserole and our first hot drinks for two days. We had made a rule when we first rowed the boat in the UK that we would not cook inside the cabin but we abandoned this after a taste of ocean life. We needed to eat something warm for a change, and gladly risked burnt eyelashes along the way.

By mid-afternoon the swell was high but more manageable. Rob was like a caged tiger, wanting to get out there and get on with it. I didn't argue and, rummaging for something to help me fix the water maker, I came across a big elastic band. This just might be the answer. I fiddled for 30 minutes, trying to sit it in the lip of the pre-filter valve case. At last I succeeded and coated it with silicone grease, put everything back together, half filled the jar with sea water and prayed to the God of all Water Makers before switching it on. A steady hum emitted from the metal and, after a nervous 5 minutes, I set the valve to run. Eureka! The first trickle of clean water ran out of the pipe and into the container.

Despite the fearful storms, and our now stinking, unwashed clothes, I felt exhilarated. "We can do this, we can do anything!" I shouted at a little sea tern that was swooping around the boat.

At 1900 hrs we crossed a time zone and were now six rather than seven hours ahead of GMT. Rob was in a musical fantasy-land with his headphones when he got hit in the small of the back by a flying fish. I bagged it to use as live bait. We hoped to row through the night and, after a delicious meal of mushroom risotto and mashed potato laced with copious amounts of Worcester sauce, we pressed on…until 2300 hrs when the capricious seas dashed our hopes once more.

I got news on the satellite phone that my old regiment, the RGBW, had won both the Army Sevens Rugby Cup and the Army Main competition. Rob and I strolled down memory lane recalling Army games at Twickenham, and who had scored the best tries.

During my time with the Regiment we never quite made it to a final, always getting knocked out in the semis. It was something that I had always dreamed of doing, as the Army Rugby Cup was a bit like the FA Cup – every unit was in the competition and with 100,000 odd men in the British Army that meant was a lot of teams and a competition that ran for several months. To hear we had won both the Sevens and the Fifteens was fantastic .

61

Mike Noel-Smith

⭐

DAY 25 – Wednesday 14th May
Location: 23:29:175S, 101:48:219E distance covered: 822nm

Having expected another hellish night, I slept like a baby, though heavy swells greeted me at first light. After Rob's welcome breakfast of coffee and a fag we were ready for battle. The low pressure on our barometer was a harbinger of more storms. Lee told us to prepare for ferocious winds of 40 or more knots.

It turned out to be another unpredictable day. We put out the sea anchor three times, only for conditions to calm. The elements were toying with us. At midday I checked the GPS to discover that we were being driven backwards.

Back home, Buffy was more worried about our mental state than the weather.

"It concerned me to hear Mike's voice faltering on the phone. He felt, probably for the first time, that he was not in charge of his destiny, and that, above everything, bothered him. He had never been in a position where he couldn't come up with a solution – feeling helpless about what was happening to him and Rob undoubtedly drove him to a place he had never been."

The sun had vanished for six days and our batteries were low. We relied on solar powered electricity and began to conserve it rigorously. This meant not using cabin or boat lights, using the laptop as little as possible and charging the satellite telephone only every two days.

The watermaker was being awkward again, getting hot around its gearbox casing and making nasty noises. I rang Southampton and spoke to an engineer who was even less helpful than the receptionist.

"It's because you are in the tropics," he suggested. Just as well for him – it meant he was thousands of miles away from my bare hands.

Despite these trials it was cheering to receive messages from friends and loved ones. Geoff emailed me more advice on catching fishing. I replied that I would as soon as the weather improved – the 20-foot waves, howling winds and menacing sharks weren't helping.

"Mike – after all those years of showing you how to catch fish on tiny rivers in Gloucestershire and huge lakes in Wales, you end up in the biggest fish zone known to man and you can't catch anything!! What are you playing at? If I were you, I'd chuck the fishing kit away and concentrate on getting to the far end as quickly as possible. Then I can take you on a refresher course."

★

DAY 26 – Thursday 15th May
Location: 23:33:828, 101:31:354E distance covered: 855nm

Another shitty day in the office! The wind was right on our nose so we didn't try to row. The pressure had bottomed out and was starting to rocket upwards. At first light, the deck looked like a battlefield, with dead flying fish and small squid everywhere. I imagined that the ferocity of the waves had stunned these creatures close to the surface and dumped them onto the deck.

We continued to be plagued by salt sores. Rashes would appear on our backs, legs and under our arms, followed by a demonic itching as the sea salt penetrated our clothing. I spent my time trying to think of anything but those itchy spots. There was never the chance to have a really good wash with fresh water and, although we treated each other with antiseptic cream, the build-up of sores was relentless. The secret was to keep the skin dry and away from salt and sun – alas, impossible in these conditions.

Lying in the cabin we spent hours discussing our fantasy World XV rugby side and the best team to play against. When we published our ruminations on our website we were deluged with emails - from our armchair-rugby playing friends and from disputatious guys and girls across the globe. It was great, distracting fun that rumbled on for days.

Here's a typical one, courtesy of Paul Matthews in Dublin

"Hi Guys. First of all well done on your rowing – what a fantastic thing to do, and an amazing experience, good luck for the rest of the trip. Now to some serious stuff – rugby. You may be built like brick shithouses and have played the game, but your knowledge is pathetic. How can you possible pick a World XV without more than 2 Irish players, and you Rob an Irishman?? Shame on you and your bigoted English ways. When you get back, me and a few of my mates extend an invitation to come to the Blackrock College RFC club bar after a Saturday game and explain this to our members. We promise not to barrack or hurt you too much…"

Mike Noel-Smith

Once again we spent the night rolling around the coffin. For our next ocean row, we decided, we would fix a flat-screen DVD player to the inside roof and maybe keep a fridge full of beers.

★

DAY 27 – Friday 16th May
Location: 23:09:981S, 100:35:850E distance covered: 907nm

The ocean was still choppy but, with the wind coming out of the South West, we decided to try to cut across the swell towards the West. We were averaging a reasonable 3.5 knots. It was still overcast and we prayed for sun to charge our dying batteries.

The electrical watermaker had died again after the elastic band snapped and so we pumped away with the handheld machine, producing just a litre an hour. It was bloody hard work - an ordeal after each two-hour rowing stag but it could keep us alive. I was relieved that we had spent our last few quid getting this machine. We'd thought we wouldn't have to take it out of its bag.

We were soaked by sidewinders and, for the first time, it was really cold on deck and in the coffin. Had we slipped so far south that we were being hit by the Southern Ocean? Thank God for my wetproof and the Norwegian shirt that Buffy had forced on me.

The sky was full of intriguing cloud formations: a mix of cirrus, high ice clouds and some anvil topped ones. All were beautiful shades of mauve and pink and precursors of bad weather, but exquisite nevertheless.

At 1930 hrs I put out the sea anchor. As we settled in the coffin an awesome storm whipped up quite the most amazing thunder and lightening show I had ever seen. The sheet lightening illuminated the entire horizon for a couple of seconds – just enough time to see the ocean waves surging forward. It reminded me vividly of the Guinness advertisement with wild horses crashing through the waters. It was fascinating to see nature at its rawest. We were getting more used to the storms, and this one was magnificent. All the same, we decided not to row since it seemed unwise to grasp three-metre, carbon fibre oars in a lightening strike.

DAY 28 – Saturday 17th May
Location: 22:54:560S, 99:55:900E distance covered: 972nm

Still no sun and Rick told us that the cloud layer extended some 2000 km towards Africa. To keep our spirits up, we decided to follow the FA Cup final on our World Service radio.

We were struggling to head westwards in the swell. The deck was littered with yet more dead and dying flying fish. Did they come in on the swell as it crashed onto the deck or did they fly at night and crash into us? You could imagine a couple chatting to each other.

"Hi Bill, how's it going?"

"Not bad Bob, these night flying lessons are great, no birds to worry about and even the big fish don't know where we are in the dark".

"Yeah, but Bill, don't you worry we might hit something on final approaches?"

"Nah, don't be stupid, what's out here to smash into, I mean we are in the middle of a bloody ocean!"

Smack.

"Sorry Bob."

We went through the morning routine of cold breakfast, hot coffee with a delightful taste of salt, a quick fag and then much grunting and swearing, pulling on the anchor.

We were averaging about 3 knots despite having to pull constantly on the right oar while the left one clutched the air. I had a sore neck from looking over my right shoulder, preparing to brace myself for big waves.

I was down to my last pack of baccy. It would last for less than a week and I wondered if Rob had any. Surely he wouldn't keep asking for mine if he didn't have any.

We had seen no other human beings now for 28 days. The odd bird came to visit us. Most dawns, a small seabird called Wilson's Petrel scampered across the wave tops, dipping its tiny feet into the water and picking up bits of plankton. Rob always gave it a cheery "Good morning". Wildlife was sparse in this part of the ocean. We had not seen any big fish for days, just a plethora of flying fish and a small green and blue creature that got wedged between the solar panels.

⭐

DAY 29 – Sunday 18th May
Location: 23:03:500S, 98:59:344E distance covered: 1020nm

A singular day of broken skies, welcome sun flashes and beautiful rainbows. We passed through one with the spectrum colours bathing the deck. Unforgettable.

I convinced myself that I could see a waterspout in the distance. I called Rob out of the cabin but we couldn't be sure. Perhaps it was really part of the weird cloud formations. Rick had warned us about waterspouts: some could rise more than 200 feet above sea level and they were always accompanied by fierce localised winds.

Feeling good and strong we cross our first 1000 nautical miles

It was a red-letter day. We crossed 1000 nautical miles at 1915 hrs, as Rob was speaking to his father, his life coach and mentor, on the satellite telephone. There were just 2250 nautical miles to go.

Rob's father told him how proud everyone was of our progress and told him not to be impatient with the mileage we were covering. We had both expected to do more and felt deflated, thinking that the folks back home would be disappointed at our lack of progress.

While rowing at 2300 hrs I sensed something off the starboard side and then saw a big dorsal fin cutting through the water four metres from my oar. A Mako shark. It stayed with me, all twelve feet of it, throughout my stag. When Rob came out, all legs and arms akimbo, I easily persuaded him that this wasn't a time to fall in. I was in awe of this beautiful but menacing beast. I wasn't afraid of it, though I thought it might attack as our oars sprayed green and yellow photo-fluorescent sparkles over the surface of the water.

But then fear gripped me when I crawled into the coffin for my rest period. I imagined the monster on the other side of two millimetres of marine plywood. Scenes from 'Jaws' filled my mind, with it chewing its way into the boat and chasing me through the cabin hatch before devouring my legs. Fortunately, it was a still night and the gentle rocking of the boat lulled me into an unexpectedly peaceful sleep.

*

CHAPTER FIVE
MAGIC

*

"The horizon is only limited by your imagination and drive"
Anon

DAY 30 – Monday 19th May
Location: 23:37:300S, 98:57:500E distance covered: 1036nm

The wind stirred during my last stag of the night and at the same time our shark disappeared. It was our coldest night yet, with my temperature gauge reading nine degrees, and I was happier to sweat at the oars than shiver inside the cabin. Rob spotted a large floating object coming towards us in the swell. Mindful that flotsam might damage the boat, we prepared to repel it with our oars. Then we identified a giant ray – it looked like a brownish manta ray - that had given up on life. It was large as a tabletop, with great lumps bitten out of it by the ocean's diverse inhabitants. Mother Nature does the perfect recycling job – nothing is wasted.

By noon the weather forced us to put out the anchor again. So frustrating. We did two interviews, with BBC Radio Portsmouth and Radio Gloucestershire who congratulated us on crossing the 1000-mile point. We tried hard to sound upbeat.

Apart from our interminable calculations and map plotting we could do little but accept being beaten up in the cabin. So we gave ourselves another challenge – making a list of the finest pubs we had visited. We put it online and got a stream of indignant replies, such as: 'How on earth could you forget the 'Little Pony' in Upper Winkington?'

DAY 31 – Tuesday 20th May
Location: 23:18:960S, 98:05:250E distance covered: 1080nm

We'd been on the ocean a month. We went from exhilarating highs as we ploughed through the awesome ocean to dispiriting lows when we made sluggish progress. We had learnt to accept that the elements ruled. All we could do was stick it out and row as hard as we could, whenever we could. This was another bad day – we were being driven backwards by the swell and, like mice on a treadmill, rowed to stand still. When not rowing we pumped hard at the mechanical watermaker for small but vital amounts. I phoned my father who was very concerned about the water maker. To him, a source of plentiful clean water in the tropics was vitally important (as indeed it was). So when Buffy told him we had a problem with the water maker he was naturally concerned.

Dad: How can you keep going without water?
Me: We have loads of water Dad – we have 50 gallons emergency water in the hold and we have a small handheld water maker to keep us topped up.
Dad: But that 50 gallons won't last forever will it?
Me: It's ok Dad. We have already started to ration ourselves in a very sensible way and that should allow us to last for at least 2 months without having to ask for help.
Dad: Why don't you ask for help?
Me: There's no need to be honest; we are still miles and days away from that moment. If we ask for help now, we lose the chance of setting a world record. There is no problem at the moment, so please don't worry Dad.
Dad: Well, you be sure that world records don't get in the way of living!

It was great to talk to him. I didn't tell him that Rob's flatmate Chris Crawford was using his contacts to see if there were any Royal Navy submarines in the vicinity that could drop off a replacement water maker. I'd thought this was a joke at first but discovered that Chris was deadly serious and willing to spend more than £10,000 to make it happen. Rob and I thought very carefully before turning down him down. It was better to spend that kind of money on

SPARKS, our children's charity, though it would have been fun to see a huge grey torpedo-shaped hull breaking the surface next to our 21-foot boat.

We hoped the wind would change overnight so we could make up lost time or at least escape the eddy that scornfully played with us. It seemed that as soon as we started making good mileage, along came a sea god to snatch it away.

✯

DAY 32 – Wednesday 21ˢᵗ May
Location: 22:54:850S, 98:31:999E distance covered: 1118nm

Back at the oars, the night seemed endless. The monotony of rowing made us feel like robots, with the very human reality of sore arms and backs. Then, at five o'clock, the wind paused as we entered that magical zone when night turns to day. I stared eastwards as the first vestiges of light crept over the wave tops, my eyes adjusting to a slowly spreading splendour. Stars faded and slipped, one by one, behind the waking sky. This was the best time of all, when you were glad to be alive, with the promise of a new day and renewed optimism after the struggle of the night.

The deck stayed dry as the sea quietened and stopped flooding through the gunwales. The only sounds were the creaking of the rollicks as I dipped the blades through light turquoise waters, and the rolling of the seat wheels on the deck track.

The light filled the eastern horizon, although behind me the night was still stubbornly unwilling to make way for the sun. An orchestra of light began with a dull red glow that joined with purple, mauve and pink hues in the brightening sky. It was time to wake Rob but I decided to wait and absorb the spectacle undisturbed. The crown of the sun's golden orb appeared and began its slow, imperial ascent. The temperature rose rapidly and the sea awoke with fish jumping everywhere. It was as if they had woken up and decided to play before getting down to the serious business of eating each other. A school of Dorado rushed past the boat like tube commuters, but more colourfully, in a magnificent blur of blues and greens. Flying fish began their graceful journeys, skimming the wave tops. In the distance, something bigger sploshed loudly. I instinctively thought of grabbing my fishing line but decided it was better just to watch it all. I told myself how blessed I was to be here, right now. However long I live, I will always treasure the beauty of those moments.

Nature had a way to reward us with beautiful images particularly at sunrise and sunset

Life on the ocean is as dangerous as it is beautiful. I had expected to grow bored with all that water, but instead I came to marvel at its majesty. It could have killed us but it exuded peace and tranquillity. We humans dash around on the land, rarely finding time to appreciate nature.

Now I felt humbled by my environment. As T.S. Eliot wrote: "The sea has many voices, many gods and many voices". With its fluid vistas – it is eternally moving, rolling, surging and twisting – and endlessly fascinating. Its colours change constantly from black to blues, greens to greys and it has an impenetrable mystery.

Even the most wondrous places I have visited on land - from mountain tops to deserts and jungles – seem almost dull and static compared with the ocean. When you are walking or climbing, you can get excited at the thought of what lies around the corner. Here I felt that every wave carried something unexpected.

My love of the sea was a new emotion. Before the trip I had spent very little time on it, occasionally swimming and wind surfing. My grandfather was in the navy a century ago but I have no record of his life at sea. I did not think that it was 'in my blood'. But it is now.

Within five minutes the light show was over as the sun overwhelmed the subtle colours and the sky settled into a light blue. I rose from my rowing seat, stretched and then fell over as a wave bashed the side of the boat.

I stumbled down to the hatch and woke Rob. Within fifteen minutes we had both breakfasted and I was tucked up on the floor of the coffin. The gentle sound of water rushing along the keel of the boat, as Rob propelled her towards Reunion Island, sent me fast asleep.

Later we did some more UK radio interviews with the World Service and Radio 5 Live. In the afternoon the weather improved as we gathered speed at last, surpassing one knot per hour. Rob called his sister to keep her up to date and Buffy urged us to give up coffee as she had detected a problem with my kidneys when sending healing to me. I supposed she was worried about our lack of drinking water.

BBC World Service: "What do you reckon people are thinking at home and do you get a chance to speak to them often?
Me: "Everyone at home is very encouraging, so that's good for our morale.

We want to go faster, but the elements are not with us. However we are confident that with the direction we are going in, it will pay dividends at the end when we have to make landfall. The whole point of keeping rigorously to our westerly line is that we end up south of Reunion in the last few days so that we can then use the prevailing winds and currents to sweep us north on to our target. If we went further north now, it would be a false gain, because we would find it difficult to get back down. So, although we find the conditions not to our liking it will be best for the end bit – that's what our router Lee Bruce is encouraging us to do.

BBC: "How do you sleep?"
Me: In shifts of 2 hours when that allows, although when the waves get too high and in the wrong direction we have to stop and put the sea anchor out. Then we are in the coffin together, which we hate, but we have to do it".

Rob was unusually positive about the upcoming weather - he thought that it might be 'almost reasonable'.

"Hey Cato. The weather looks good, let's rip that ocean up!"

"What's with this upbeat mood, Alexander?" (Alexander was my nickname for him – he liked to think he was the young Alexander the Great)

"My reckoning is that we have had the worst that the ocean can throw at us, now it's our turn to put some big miles in."

"Mate, this ocean has a lot more nastiness to put out if it wants to. We just have to be mentally prepared for plenty of setbacks I reckon. But you are right, the forecast is good, we are fit and well, we can definitely put a big chunk off our target over the next few days, but don't think we have seen the last of the weather."

"Cato, I don't care what's likely to come, it cannot be any worse than what we've been through."

"I hear what you're saying, but just don't get too optimistic, that's all. Come on let's row together."

I was starting to smell again and decided to try washing in salt water. The salt made it impossible to work up a good soapy lather but the activity was at least mentally refreshing.

We still relished the excitement of downloading emails from everyone back at home and beyond. These were a huge morale booster.

From Denis (my brother)
To: TRANSVenture

Just to let you know, the weather has got better here, so it must be ok with you?! We all think you are doing exceptionally well, and I am trying to organize potential dates to bring a little welcome party out to Reunion to greet you in. When do you think you will arrive given your current average daily mileages? I think sometime late June or early July. What do you think? Everyone is well here, Dad especially who asks after you every time we speak, I really must try and teach him about the internet so he can follow your progress. We are still all waiting for an account of fish caught – strikes me you have either lost it or were never any good…

Row hard and God speed, Denis

Rob's back and shoulder were troubling him and he started taking painkillers and taking more of the Bach flower remedies that Buffy had given to us. He spoke to Lee who agreed with Rick for once, saying that the weather should be okay until Monday – great news.

★

DAY 33 – Thursday 22nd May
Location: 22:39:520S, 97:56:400E distance covered: 1166nm

So much for the forecasts. It started raining at midnight and got steadily worse. I gave up rowing at 0330 hrs because it was lashing my eyes too painfully. Nevertheless, the sea was quite calm and so, instead of putting out the anchor, I set the rudder on a fixed bearing and dived into the coffin.

Rob looked up quizzically, as if to say what the hell are you doing?

I explained that I would stay awake monitoring the radar reflector but not sit outside getting drenched. 'Slacker!' he mumbled and went back to sleep. We were flying along at three knots and, short of hitting another boat, we would be fine. It was the first time that I had let the elements take charge in this way and I was pleased with the results.

During the day the waters became porridge-like again and we struggled to maintain one knot per hour. Then the wind picked up and we got enthusiastically back into our rowing routine through the night.

Nick emailed us a story from The Times. A man on an inflatable lobster had rescued a young girl, who was blown out to sea on a set of inflatable teeth. A coastguard spokesman commented that 'this sort of thing is all too common nowadays'.

★

DAY 34 – Friday 23rd May
Location: 22:54:215S, 97:08:950E distance covered: 1211nm

At dawn the wind and swell were still pushing us onwards. Overnight something had grabbed at the fishing line and hooks that I had put out but only some fish's mouths were left behind. Once again I had unwittingly fed the sharks. I was determined to catch something with my excellent kit and Rob's endless leg pulling made me keener still. The fish would provide a welcome and nutritious change to our diet. However, while I hooked plenty, I couldn't get even one on deck. It was clear by now that we were being followed at all times, often imperceptibly, by small blue sharks and white tips that decapitated my supper before I could reel it in.

In frustration I cast a fish-head with a couple of big hooks back into the sea … and it caught onto a prowling shark. It was a very stupid thing to do. Even if I could drag the five-foot shark on board, how on earth would I kill it? When the shark bit, it ripped the line into the flesh of my right hand, causing me to drop everything in anguish. The beast dragged the line for about 30 metres and snapped it like cotton. It was the first and last time that I tried fishing for sharks.

We had covered a reasonable 48 nautical miles on Thursday, crossing into another time zone. With many more days like this we would reach Reunion Island by mid- July. When my hand stopped bleeding I decided to check the underside of the boat for barnacles, wondering if they were slowing our progress even as we were pushed ahead by the swell.

Rob agreed to stand guard with the shotgun and we tried a little target practice first.

It was a hefty weapon with a hell of a kick but we were hopeless shots. We missed all the biodegradable cardboard boxes that we had set bobbing on the water as our boat swept along. The explosions rudely disturbed the peace as our shots bounced into the distance like skimming stones.

I climbed into the water and saw that the port side rudder line, running from the deck along the side of the boat and sternwards to the rudder itself, was badly frayed. It had to be replaced immediately. If it snapped we would lose control of the steering and, if the side of the boat turned to face incoming waves, we would capsize. It was tricky work, as I had to keep pace with the boat. We had calculated that we were now in the deepest part of the ocean. If I drowned, I wondered, would I sink all the way to the bottom? At more than 5,000 metres it was a greater distance down than the height of any of the mountains that I had climbed.

After ten minutes work I hauled myself back on deck and asked Rob if I could take over with the shotgun while he had a swim!

Wild Waters in the Roar

*While I clean the barnacles under the Rob stands guard!
boat Rob stands guard with his trusty shotgun*

I was delighted by our progress after the fearsome storms and the crisis with the watermaker. We were going to make it.

I began to recall how, just a few months before - after we had secured our boat and agreed to adopt SPARKS (the childhood meningitis trust) as our charity – we still had no proper funding. No money, no expedition – what would we do?

Then Scipio, an angel in a City suit, came to our rescue. He is a successful banker with celebrity connections who insists on staying anonymous – so we named him after the legendary Roman general who routed Hannibal.

Rob knew Scipio and asked for his help in securing us some corporate sponsorship. Shortly before Christmas, over lunch in a smart City restaurant, Scipio told Rob that the potential sponsor he was chasing had gone cold and would give us very little or nothing. Then he suddenly announced that he was putting £25,000 of his own money into our project.

Rob was stunned.

"What can we do for you in return?" he asked.

"Just go and do it!"

What a man, and what great vision and faith in us. We would not let him down, whatever the obstacles. We felt filled with the great British spirit of adventure and daring.

After Scipio's donation we got even more vital support - from our families and friends, Harry's primary school (which kindly insisted on buying our oars), Betfair (which became our title sponsor) and Cathay Pacific (which flew TRANSVenture to Australia at reduced cost). And, with more media coverage, donations to SPARKS came in from all over the country. It was all systems go.

★

DAY 35 – Saturday 24th May
Location: 23:16:196S, 96:18:860E distance covered: 1273nm

A cavalry charge of a hundred-odd flying fish gave us an awesome display, hurtling through the air before diving and then re-appearing on the other side of our boat. Excitedly I grabbed my fishing line, keen to catch whatever was chasing them. But despite using lots of different lures, I could persuade nothing to bite.

We read emails confirming that my father, my eldest sister Carol and her husband Chris would arrive on Reunion Island on the 8th July and stay until the 18th. Rob's parents were coming too. For us to get there and meet them on the 15th we had to cover a minimum of 38 nautical miles per day for the next 52 days. It would be hard going, and there was bound to be more bad weather, but we were full of optimism.

I was less pleased to discover that my tobacco was almost completely gone and Rob finally confessed that he had none stashed away. We thought about summoning that Royal Navy submarine with fresh supplies but decided to struggle on.

Then we got the news that Simon Chalk, a fellow – or, should I say, rival - rower had been forced to abandon his Indian Ocean odyssey. Hats off to him for rowing solo for more than 100 days. But I have to confess he had irritated us with claims that we had somehow cheated by getting a tow to our start-line.

While Rob's back pain was easing, my left shoulder ached constantly, probably as a result of pulling in the anchor every day and rowing mostly on the left side. I strapped on the magnetic packs that my sister Carol had given me. Magnetic therapy is meant to increase the flow of newly oxygenated blood over an area of injury and remove the build-up of toxins.

Carol is a former nurse and health visitor. She had come across the power of magnotherapy when she was living in Plymouth and, along with her husband; Chris (a GP) did a lot of research into their healing properties. She recommended that I wear a small watch type bracelet to help with motion sickness and gave me a couple of larger back straps to assist if I had any difficulty with my back during the row.

Certainly the small watch bracelet helped me – I was not getting sea sick, and the other ones were great for my back when the muscles got over-used. I would put them on for a 2- hour 'blast' when I had my time off – they seemed to work. It may have been the power of positive thinking of course, but anything is worth a try when you are in chronic pain.

We did an excellent night's hard graft and were rewarded by another beautiful dawn.

☆

DAY 36 – Sunday 25th May
Location: 23:33:370S, 95:19:421E distance covered: 1338nm

The sea and swell was still with us and the winds blew at 12-15 knots – perfect conditions. We were determined to put in another 50-nautical-mile day. After five days of rowing almost non-stop the tiredness really hit me during the night stags. It was worst on cloudy, starless nights when all I could see was the dull, green glow from the GPS, which cast an eerie soporific spell over me. But it was far better to row than to swelter in the coffin - the temperatures had soared again. Tonight the sky was clear and I became mesmerised by the shooting stars, some of which I tracked across the sky for several seconds. They appeared in all directions. I idly wondered if they might break through the earth's atmosphere and crash fierily into the ocean … maybe into our patch of the ocean? The display kept me awake and concentrating throughout the session and I was rewarded with proof from the GPS readout that we had completed 65 nautical miles in 24 hours.

When I closed my eyes in the cabin I visualised the tiny port in Reunion that I had reconnoitred the year before – a stunning setting with volcano cliffs and two huge waterfalls cascading into the sea. Aged fishermen set out from this tiny inlet in their wooden boats. I pictured our arrival. We had anchored during the night some 10 miles from the shore so that we could arrive in daylight. We tidied up the boat and donned our only clean t-shirts. As dawn brightened the sky, a boat-full of our mates came out to urge us on. A helicopter carrying my father and Rob's parents buzzed above us and we talked to them on our VHF radio. We put out our giant GB flag to fly off the stern as we powered our way into the port. Cheers, laughter, tears and hugs. An epic arrival.

*

CHAPTER SIX
TIDE OF FORTUNE

*

"The daily grind of hard work gets a person polished"
Anon

DAY 37 – Monday 26th May
Location: 23:29:817S, 94:14:991E distance covered: 1395nm

It was a Bank Holiday in the UK and we received no emails. Chris, our project manager, usually forwarded them to us and must have gone away for a long weekend. This was irritating because we had grown to depend on the warmth of encouraging words from around the globe. Rob would have a word with Chris, explaining that we needed a constant watch over our website and a point of contact for our families and friends.

The climate was still kind, gently pushing us in the right direction, and it was less blisteringly hot on deck. We had kept rowing around the clock and made a very satisfying 64 nautical miles. My shoulder still hurt despite the magnets: I probably wasn't drinking enough water to purge the toxins. Both Rob and I were feeling the muscular strain of constantly pumping the handheld water maker.

Lee called, warning that the weather could turn bad from Wednesday night. We needed to cover as much ocean as possible while we could. Later in the day, clouds gathered in the Northern skies and water again invaded the deck through the scuppers.

★

DAY 38 – Tuesday 27th May
Location: 23:33:672S, 93:22:680E distance covered: 1450nm

The seas were still mostly running with us, and so with occasional adjustments cutting across the waves, we managed to stay westerly. We crossed 1400 nautical miles at almost 0930 hrs.

Buffy sent me a long email. She was back from a rugby tournament with Isabelle and Harry, where she had met a woman whose husband was joining the Ward Evans Atlantic Ocean rowing race. What a small world it was.

As the sun descended and we enjoyed supper together on deck, we witnessed a rare and delightful optical phenomenon: the green flash. For a moment, the sun radiated green light across the horizon before it vanished. With our pure air and uncluttered view, we were in one of the best possible places for this. I may never see it again but the memory will endure until my toes turn up – toes that by this point in the trip had already endured a lifetime's soaking in water. My swollen feet would not have been out of place in the trenches of the Somme.

We carried on through the watery night, making good progress. Rob thought he heard a whale blowing, far away to our port. I wish we had seen one close up. Peering into the inky darkness, searching for the planet's largest mammal, we felt tiny and distant from our loved ones. I collapsed in the coffin when I finished my stag at 0200 hours. Headphones on, I slumbered to the electric guitar of Funkadelic's 'Maggot Brain'.

★

DAY 39 – Wednesday 28th May
Location: 23:52:700S, 92:50:700E distance covered: 1487nm

The wind changed in the night and we were fighting to stay westwards against seas pushing us to the south. Riled waters crashed over the deck, grabbing anything not tied down – farewell to a wooden spoon, a plastic plate and a book on speaking French. Nonetheless, by breakfast time we had made a splendid 30 nautical miles in 12 hours.

Rob gave Chris a bollocking, which I doubt he appreciated, about being available 24/7. It was my nephew Henry's birthday and I decided to call him from the middle of the Indian Ocean – that should give him something to tell his schoolmates. Buffy called to say that Will had won a speech day prize for PE at Monmouth Boys School. Isabelle also emailed me about her exploits in the rugby tournament. I was immensely proud of them.

In the afternoon the wind shifted again, now trying to force us southeastwards. Lee warned that we were close to an eddy that would drive us backwards. The conditions deteriorated and we put out the anchor. It was nine days since we had last stopped rowing. We stayed in the coffin all night while a spectacular rain and thunderstorm played outside. The sky was ablaze with lightening for hours. With each strike, explosions of white light penetrated the lewmar hatches and danced in the dark corners of the coffin – like an old horror movie. The rain was so loud that I feared it would smash into the cabin.

Spanish International FM called at 0130 hrs and Marcus, a friendly Irishman, interviewed me. It was fantastic that his audience of ex-pats were raising money for our charity.

Breakfast was a soggy affair. A wave snatched a microwave breakfast dish from Rob's hands just as he was putting a spoonful of cereal into his mouth. I found this hilarious. After a scowl from Rob, I tried to control myself but to no avail. We both burst out laughing. I spoke to Lee on the satellite phone. He said things should calm down soon.

✭

DAY 40 – Thursday 29th May
Location: 23:16:636S, 92:35:206E distance covered: 1554nm

At last - 1500 miles! We were again 'cross graining' – rowing against the current - in big seas and getting plenty of soakings. The swell was reaching 10 metres, much higher than a double-decker bus. In between our rowing stags, we each pumped four buckets of fresh water to make up for the previous night. The solar panels on the roof were pockmarked in testimony to the power of the rain.

My mind wandered homeward, as I tried to imagine everyone doing their favourite things: Will and Isabelle playing rugby, Harry swimming, Buffy massaging at the nearby therapy centre.

Rowing was tough today and we regarded any progress as good. We had covered 67 nautical miles in twenty-four hours - excellent in these appalling conditions.

I did another interview with Meridian TV in Portsmouth. They were very keen to hear about our progress, especially since our charity money was going to a foundation at the local university. Stuart Ross was generating tons of publicity for us: it seemed that whenever we switched on the phone someone wanted to know how we were doing. We were very grateful for such good coverage. To be honest, though, it was also a pain. It was hard to sound upbeat all the time, especially in response to inane questions like, 'Don't you feel tired?' or 'How are you feeling?'

By nightfall, drained by all the rowing and pumping - not to mention the media work - I crawled into the cabin, yearning for sleep to renew my spirit and body. The temperatures had plunged and I tried using my wet sarong as an extra layer for warmth. I was too exhausted to care about the dampness. At least the next day the weather should improve.

✮

DAY 41 – Friday 30th May
Location: 23:07:745S, 91:25:974E distance covered: 1631nm

We made substantial headway overnight. Chris forwarded an email from Kenneth Crutchlow, founder of the Ocean Rowing Society, which said that we could not maintain a daily average of more than 38 nautical miles. Mr Crutchlow might be good at statistics but we were determined to prove him wrong.

The seas were big and fast, but they were more or less heading our way and we hung on as the swell powered us along.

Awesome rainbows graced the skies as the sheets of rain tangled with shafts of sunlight. ABC Perth Radio called in for a lunchtime interview. They seemed amazed that we had got so far and this boosted us despite our frazzled bodies.

I was rowing in the fading light when a giant pair of wings came over the top of the swell towards us. Every time the bird adjusted its course, it seemed that those wings must dip into the water. But they didn't. Despite its disproportionately large head, the albatross was a supremely graceful beast, skimming over the wave tops and our boat and away into the distance. After 10 minutes it flew back towards us and I yelled to Rob. Mindful of Coleridge's poem, I was pleased that he emerged from the cabin without his shotgun! We were escorted for a whole hour by the creature with the longest wind-span on earth. Then it glided off into the night and we decided that perhaps it would be waiting for us at Reunion. We felt sure that it was a good omen. We were tired but hugely satisfied with our progress, which seemed to get better each day.

★

DAY 42 – Saturday 31st May
Location: 22:52:500S, 90:01:500E distance covered: 1690nm

We kept rowing through the night. It was like being on the fastest, nastiest ride at Alton Towers – only free of charge, with no need to queue. We had managed 77 nautical miles in 24 hours - our best yet.

After breakfast I sent an email to John Foster at Lloyds TSB and had a good hard think about how best to use the publicity surrounding the expedition's to help build our management training business. Our charity was doing well and we also had to think about ourselves. I kept my brain sharp by designing a business game about making the right decisions at the right times. It involved building blocks and plastic tubing – a sort of child's game for adults.

The rollercoaster ride continued. We were almost on autopilot as TRANSVenture crashed along, with and through the building swell. Experts would describe the sea state as 'confusing'. We had no idea where the swell was coming from or going to - as if Poseidon was playing with a turbo-charged electric mixer.

We were making our all-time best speeds of up to 15.2 knots in this mother of all rides. Rick called with the cheery news that these conditions could last a week. At this rate we might reach the finish point at the end of June. I just hoped that our relatives and friends could get there early.

I called home and spoke to everyone. It was great for my morale but again it reminded me how much I missed them all. Still, by hook or by crook we were set for a joyous reunion in Reunion.

It was showing all the signs of being an 80-mile day but we still had to stay alert on each stag or our dreams could be smashed. As the afternoon waned, some extreme rain put an edge on our worries. My mind raced with the wind: 'Am I in control?' 'Did anyone predict these bloody nightmare conditions?' The rain lashed us horizontally and visibility dropped to the level of mountaintop 'white outs' - when you can see no further than the end of your nose. The bow and the immediate waves were the only things in view.

Near the end of my stag I was looking forward to retreating to the cabin where Rob was preparing an energy-rich, gastronomic delight. Suddenly a big-handed wave swept me up in the air and smashed my head against the gunwale. Than another wave grabbed me and dumped me unceremoniously into the well.

I had never experienced such violence in my whole life. Sure, I had been hurt often before, but never with such unexpectedly brutal force. After the shock, awful pain filled my head and my nose throbbed excruciatingly. I noticed blood and my eyes danced as I looked out to sea.

As I crawled into the cabin, water rushed in through the open hatch wrecking Rob's meal. He swore but then looked shocked by my dishevelled look and bloody nose.

"You okay mate?"

"Yeah, I just didn't see that coming!"

I am a man and so of course I was 'okay' though, in truth, I was in agony. I rummaged around for Buffy's rescue remedy, but it only made me feel more light-headed, probably because of its alcohol base. While the pain around my nose ebbed, the throbbing in my head intensified like a building storm. I said nothing to Rob but I knew I was badly hurt. Later, when I dragged myself out on deck to discover that the sea anchor was lost, it felt as if my spinning brain would burst out of my skull.

✯

DAY 43 – Sunday 01 June
Location: 23:09:500S, 89:42:200E (mileage not taken)

We put out the spare anchor just before midnight. The main one had been ripped out the bow of the boat. It was chaos on deck with broken kit, tangled ropes and water everywhere. Rob came out with me to ensure everything was battened down. My head was pounding and my eye kept flickering. Everything seemed to have slowed down and I was operating at a quarter of my normal speed. It took five minutes of fumbling to attach to my harness as my fingers were resisting the messages from my brain. Simple acts had become complicated and difficult. We tried to row again a couple of hours later but realised after 20 minutes that we were totally out of control – though, amazingly, we did two and a half miles in this time.

With all the pitching about, breakfast in the cabin was a shambles. There was food everywhere and we were soaked. The seas were horrendous and the waves kept smashing onto the deck. Rob threw our coffee cups away when the well filled up with water. He had mistakenly put them in our bale-out bucket and so they went over the side as he started to bale. It was a little thing, but he was distraught. I told him it was no big deal. We could improvise I was sure.

I spoke to Buffy, and told her about my accident. I could sense from her voice that she wasn't happy as she told me to take rescue remedy and arnica and to get Rob to do all the manual work for a while. I tried to sound brave for her, but I honestly felt like bursting into tears. Rob needed me to pull my weight and not be an invalid out here in the storms.

Buffy recalls the telephone call: "The weather was warm enough for some of our friends to enjoy a BBQ at Pool Farm. We were celebrating Mike and Rob's passing the halfway point in their row. There had been lots of funny emails between TRANSVenture and us about the best venue and the dress code, but we made do with a BBQ in our garden. When Mike called me, I knew something was amiss. He always called unexpectedly when something was wrong and he wanted moral support from home. His voice was more distant and tired than usual, but I put that to the back of my mind - no use worrying. They had been speeding along, as much as you can on a rowing boat on an ocean, and so our spirits were high. Mike told me he had been "taken out" by a freak wave and banged his head against the side of the boat. But he was okay. I told him to take some rescue remedy and arnica for the shock and bruising and got back to the BBQ".

In the night we turned turtle. We'd experienced this before but it was just as scary. 'What happens if the boat doesn't right?' I asked myself. Looking out through the forward hatch was bad for morale. We were enveloped by sea, with drips seeping through the hatch seal. Then we were hit by a benign wave turning us upright again and we both prayed a silent 'thank you' to God. My head was burning now and Chris called to say I had to come off the boat. The chilling winds and lashing rain made everything worse.

☆

DAY 44 – Monday 02 June
Location: 23:26:590S, 89:29:081E (no mileage taken)

We were at the mercy of a ferocious storm, with torrential rain bursts, winds surging at more than 40 knots and prodigious seas. It was very wet and miserable in the coffin. We both felt depressed, especially Rob, since the latest advice from Chris was that we should both quit. We could do nothing but sit it out. Our weatherman Lee was worried that it could get worse overnight as we entered the eye of the storm. Apparently I kept passing out. I remember vomiting a couple of times. Rob spoke to Buffy who was reassuring. She remembers the call:

"At about 7 am I got another unscheduled call from TRANSVenture. This time it was Rob, who was worried about Mike. Since Mike's call the day before he had been falling in and out of consciousness, with a crushing headache and problems with his eyes. To top it all they were in another bad storm. He asked what I thought. What could I think? It doesn't sound good, was all I could say.

I called the girls to send some healing to Mike. When I called Jill she burst into tears. She had been woken in the middle of the night with an excruciating headache and she knew it wasn't hers. Jill was relieved in a way to know where her headache had come from, but the intensity of it and Mike's situation brought great anguish. She was not happy about his condition at all. This was not the first time Mike's pain had manifested in a healing friend of mine; I seemed to avoid his physical pain.

Before I managed to get through to the other girls Rob phoned again to say they had been advised to abort the row, "how did I feel about it". Relief, and that I was sure it was the right thing considering Mike's condition. Aborting the row was not the end to their dilemma: how, when and by what means were they going to be rescued? No use in worrying. I lit a candle for their safe return and Mike's healing.

I asked for guidance and opened my book 'Love is in the earth': the page opened at Petrified Palm, which can assist with head injuries and has been used to treat disorders of the optic nerve and light sensitivity. It was what I had been looking for, so I asked that these vibrations be sent to Mike and left the book open by the candles I had burning. I called Cath, a cranial-sacral therapist who worked in the area and asked if she could please send Mike some distant healing. I felt Mike needed someone who understood the skull and the energies that lie within. She didn't know me, although we had a mutual friend.

It dawned on me what had been troubling me. I had not been able to visualise being reunited with Mike on Reunion Island. I had been there, I could picture the place where they were hoping to come in, yet try as I might I could not receive clear images of their completing their row there. Now I knew why. I reassured the children that Daddy was going to be okay. It wasn't difficult as it's honestly how I felt. I also took great strength from being reassured by my healing friends that everything would be fine and Mike and Rob would be rescued".

*

CHAPTER SEVEN
DISASTER

*

"Adversity does not build character…it reveals it"
Anon

Rob writes:

From nowhere an enormous force hit the boat with a resounding crash, pushing me against the roof of the cabin. The next thing I knew, the entire cabin and, perhaps more importantly, the saucepan containing the lamb casserole, was full of seawater. The boat shuddered upright and then I saw Mike. He looked bloody and bedraggled.

"You ok?" I shouted.

"Bastard wave almost knocked me out," he mumbled "Let's get the storm anchor out and stop. I think the storm may be coming quicker than anticipated".

I noticed the bump that was swelling over Mike's right eye.

"Blimey, you sure you're ok?"

"Yeah, just a bit of a knock, but that wave really had some force in it. Picked me up a good four feet and hurled me back down. Glad I had my harness on, otherwise I would have been off. Thing I don't understand is that it came from a completely different direction from all the other waves. Sorry".

I knew that Mike was a hard bugger but he had taken a massive knock and I made a mental note to keep an eye on him over the next few hours in case he had minor concussion. It can take a while to show.

The night following the freak wave was uncomfortable by anyone's standards. It must have been dreadful for Mike. Although the cabin had emptied of water, all of our personal kit was sodden and, with the rain pelting outside, there was no chance of drying it. Lee had warned us the rain would last a long time. The rain-band stretched two hundred miles to our north and four hundred miles to our south and it was moving so slowly that we were going to be stuck with it for at least another week. Oh yes, that was good for morale!

As we munched on our substitute for the chef's lamb casserole – a couple of energy bars – I quizzed Mike about the size and, more importantly, the direction of the wave. It appeared that it was indeed a rogue wave, hitting the boat at an angle of about seventy degrees to the main direction of the sea. It had smashed us as Mike tweaked the rudder. He had felt an ominous presence over his left shoulder and was suddenly airborne, heading for a bang on the head against our handrail.

Later we learned more about this force of nature. Once dismissed as a nautical myth freak waves – rising as high as ten-storey blocks – are now thought to be the main cause of large ships sinking. More than 200 supertankers and container ships longer than 200 metres have sunk in the past two decades. The European Space Agency satellites have helped establish the widespread existence of rogue waves and are studying their origins. Multiple waves can intersect and add up to a much larger one. Currents and eddy systems can also contribute to their formation. The worst thing is that their direction is wholly unexpected, often catching mariners off guard. The shocking scenes in the Hollywood movie "The Perfect Storm" are realistic.

As we chatted in the cold and wet of the cabin, Mike seemed okay considering what had happened, though he complained of a severe headache and was convinced that he had broken his nose, which wouldn't stop bleeding. He was more worried that his right eye felt like it was fluttering all the time, open or shut, though I could see no movement in it. I decided to call Chris and my parents in the morning to describe the symptoms and seek further advice.

As I bailed out water from the well I noticed that Mike's head had split the reinforced marine plywood handrail in two. Bugger waiting until the morning!

I phoned Chris to alert him, in case Mike got worse, and to explain about the dire weather. I also tried calling my sister, but she was on the Car Ferry from Cowes to Southampton in beautiful flat sea conditions.

Chris wasn't too keen on being woken in the small hours back in the UK and predictably he told me to wait until the morning to see how things developed.

Wild Waters in the Roar

I called Rick, back in Carnarvon. He was worried, not only about Mike, but also the likelihood that the storm would get worse. He said he would tell the Australian sea rescue services of our position, so that they could react quickly if necessary.

At around 2200 hours, all hell broke loose outside. And then it happened. A huge 'whooshing' sound, followed by a massive crash and we went upside down. Kit flew in all directions and Mike and I ended lying on the roof, watching the little spurts of water coming through our two 'waterproof' hatches. Amazingly, the marine batteries had not de-coupled and our small cabin light still shone brightly, projecting a ghostly scene. We looked at each other, said nothing and prayed that our self-righting boat would right itself. Outside the main hatch window, the sea was bubbling and frothing like the inside of a washing machine. I knew that it would be a nightmare opening the hatch and we would have to allow all the water to flood in before trying to escape. I also knew that opening that hatch would mean the end of our journey.

Mike found the grab bag and I got our lifejackets. We struggled to put them on upside down. I thought about activating my Emergency Position-Indicating Radio Beacon but decided to give it another couple of minutes. Bang! Another wave hit us and suddenly we were upright again. We lurched around like manic cowboy riders at a rodeo.

Mike said he was going outside to check our anchor. I didn't want him to go but he was being plain obstinate and disappeared into the night with his head torch.

He returned soaked through and said that our storm anchor had been ripped off by the waves. He could not deploy the spare one as it was twisted and he needed my help. Crawling out into the maelstrom, I was scared as I tried to hook on my safety harness while being thrown around. The entire deck seemed to be under water and struggling to drain itself. Up at the bow end we spent ten minutes freeing the spare anchor by unravelling the cord that had whipped around our navigation mast. At one stage we looked at each other and just burst out laughing. We were as far into the Indian Ocean and away from land as you could be, the waves were unbelievable, we had turned upside down, and here we were pathetically trying to unravel a piece of string that might save our lives.

Eventually we untangled it and threw the anchor out into the sea. We watched as the rope peeled away and the anchor started to take the boat round into the waves. Mike had said ages ago that he wasn't confident about its performance and, sure enough, it didn't appear to be up to the job in these huge waters. We realised that the chain attached to the parachute end wasn't heavy enough to pull it below the thrashing water. We needed more weight. Apart from our marine batteries the only likely candidate was my shotgun. Heavy hearted, I crawled back to the cabin while Mike hauled in the 75 metres of rope. I was gutted. I had bought the gun in Carnarvon and was fond of our shark and pirate deterrent. But it might do the job and we had to be anchored soon. After much fumbling about with cord, the gun was duly strapped on and thrown overboard. Thankfully the anchor went straight down and we were riding into the waves once again.

Mike crawled back inside the cabin and collapsed in a heap. Pulling in the anchor had exhausted him. I wasn't feeling too good either. I couldn't help thinking, 'What happens if this anchor gets ripped off like the last one?' We had no third anchor. I munched an energy bar, dozed occasionally and waited for daylight.

Things looked bad. Mike was hurt, lying with matted blood in his beard and a huge swelling on his head. I was sure that the boat was damaged and we were going to be in this crap for at least another 72 hours. We were completely at the mercy of the elements and they could take us down at any time. Of course we had always known that the ocean was a dangerous place, but something had changed. Mike wasn't sitting up joking or putting a bright complexion on things as he always did. It felt like I was alone now and totally responsible for his well-being. And the responsibility extended further than this little boat of ours. It reached thousands of miles back to a house where his wife and family were waiting - probably right now - for reassurance that he would be okay. It was frightening.

*

CHAPTER EIGHT
INCREDIBLE THINGS

*

"Within me is infinite power, before me is endless possibility. Around me is boundless opportunity…why should I fear?"

DAY 45
… no location or mileage recorded from this point

At daybreak the bleak reality of our situation became clearer. We huddled in the cabin, cold and miserable. Our dream was collapsing.

Rob called the UK and spoke to a doctor whose advice was unequivocal. My head injury needed urgent professional attention. Our medical training before the trip was no use in this situation. We had to abandon the row.

I felt bloody awful with headaches and shivers, probably a broken nose and, worryingly, my eyes kept flickering involuntarily. I also kept losing consciousness. It was like going under anaesthetic for an operation. I knew I was going to pass out and couldn't stop it. I was cold but with a fine layer of sweat on my forehead and palms. I felt nauseous and then everything around me became quiet and remote. I couldn't hear Rob talking – he was just mouthing at me. Then he'd shake me by the arm and say, "You alright? You've just passed out again". At first I didn't believe him. Nothing had changed. I was still in the same position, on the same boat, looking at the same person. Rob faithfully kept a record of this and relayed the information to a neuro-surgeon in Britain. In the next 48 hours I lost consciousness 28 times, for periods of between 30 seconds and seven minutes. Every time I came to, I vomited. Usually I managed to get my head out of the hatch but Rob gave me a bucket for when I couldn't.

I spoke to Buffy again. Her voice was reassuring, cutting through the mayhem outside as clearly as if she was sitting beside me. She was calmly adamant. Enough was enough. We had to take the medical advice and abide by the wishes of our loved ones. I knew she was right and didn't even think of disagreeing. With my wife and children at home, how could I risk another smash to my head and end up with brain damage or worse? But it was still very hard to accept.

I handed the satellite telephone to Rob and we looked at each other in despair. The next call should be to Rick in Carnarvon to tell him to alert the Maritime Rescue Authority.

At first Rob didn't seem to believe what the doctors were saying. "Are you absolutely sure you can't go on?" he asked. It was a daft thing to say. He had spoken to the doctors and it wasn't me making the decision.

Tears were in our eyes as we were lost in our individual thoughts. Then Rob bravely announced that he was going to soldier on after I had been picked up. He was going to do it for us. He was not going to be beaten. "Mate, don't be a bloody fool", I said.

It didn't take me long to convince him. The boat was damaged, the water-maker was broken and he had 1,500 miles ahead. Despite his toughness it was highly unlikely that he could do it on his own. We were a team. We had gone through hell and high water together and we would finish together. Rob called his sister Clare and she said the same as Buffy had to me.

Then he made the call to Rick to tell him we were stopping and ask if any ship was close enough to pick us up. The chart showed us to be near the middle of the ocean and at the furthest point from land. We were terribly isolated. Rick explained that the closest vessels, a Liberian oil tanker and an Italian mine sweeper, were about 500 miles away and neither of them could guarantee us medical support. The HMAS Newcastle, an Australian frigate, had a doctor and helicopter on board.

However, she was on fisheries protection duty some 1200 miles away near the Cocos Islands and it would take her up to four days to reach us. The Maritime Rescue Authority instructed the HMAS Newcastle to steam to our aid.

The storm outside seemed to be getting worse, or maybe it was our imagination. It was depressing sitting in the cabin listening to the crump of the waves against our hull and the mad rattling of our wind direction flag on the cabin roof. We made a few calls home to reassure everyone that things were not so bad, or maybe it was to reassure ourselves. Looking through the hatch at the wild ocean we felt once again vulnerable to nature. It seemed like the worst time in my life. My nadir. I thought back to other bad experiences.

In the army, I had always felt low when my men got hurt, and sometimes badly wounded, on operations. They were my people and I felt responsible. I painfully learnt over time that you cannot always guarantee the safety of your men, no matter how hard you try. When they do get hurt, it is your responsibility to make sure they are well looked after and that their next of kin are supported.

When my mother was dying of cancer, I had been to her care home every day and she was pleased to see me. On the day she died, my eldest sister called to say that she was fading rapidly. I was an hour away and drove like the wind to reach her. But she died two minutes before I walked through the door. I guess it was not meant to be for me to be with her when she died. Pondering on the end of our adventure, I felt I had let the side down and I was gripped with guilt. People's hopes of our success would be dashed. I am a very positive person and this rubs off on everyone I meet. If I failed, I could imagine people feeling sad, or even disappointed and let down. My family had placed so much faith in us. I remembered my brother writing a letter to our siblings. He wrote that, apart from Dad's heroic wartime experiences as a fighter pilot, this was the most spectacular thing anyone in our family had attempted. They should all support the venture financially and be justly proud.

I do not like to fail at anything. I have always been hugely competitive - in school and army sports and in exams. Even as a cook I like to get a great result. This experience had challenged my life ethos and it was agonizing as it pierced me to my core, my inner being, my soul. I imagined some of the public and media getting a kick out of an expedition failure. It's the sort of thing we Brits like to do – give ourselves a hard time.

How many would be in their chairs smirking with an 'I told you so' attitude? I felt guilty for Rob. We had shared everything on this journey starting from his first call to me over a year ago. Part of me said I was destroying his dream.

However I also knew that if it were Rob lying here smashed up, I would do everything to make sure he recovered. Sod the journey – we would always have another day. I flipped through the book Buffy had given me. It was called Bag of Jewels, written by Susan Hayward. It had motivational and spiritual quotations and it was my favourite and most thumbed book on the boat. Every page had a little hand written quote or line from a family member or friend. These were a joy to read and I smiled thinking of those who wrote them.

Then I realised that I was simply feeling sorry for myself. There was nothing else to feel guilty about. Destiny had chosen this for us.

It wasn't the first time I'd felt in the hands of fate. I remembered when my elder brother Dennis and I were stuck in a blizzard on top of a glacier on the French/Swiss border. We were sheltering in a tiny hole we had dug out of snow and ice that clung precariously to the mountainside for two days while avalanches crashed all around us. We survived. So would Rob and I. We would become better and stronger people through the experience.

Lying in the cabin and looking across at Rob, I knew that this challenge was not over. Someday we would come back and finish the job. This was a chapter in a book that one day we would finish. We would get through this. We would hold our heads high, knowing that we had done our very best.

We were helped by a barrage of supportive emails from around the world. My favourite was from Scipio, our mentor, supporter, benefactor and good friend. He wrote this the day after we decided to abandon the row:

"Rob and Mike. Heroism comes in many forms and guises…but one knows a hero when one see one…and you two are heroes to me for what you have done, for what you have driven yourselves to achieve and for what you have shown to all of us about dedication, hard work, commitment, enthusiasm and teamwork.

The crew of Apollo 13 were heroes even though they did not achieve their goal of walking on the moon – they and all the people in their support team back in Houston met a crisis and delivered the ultimate goal – to get home safely. The great mountaineers are those who know when not to climb. The great soldiers are those who know the difference between bravery and recklessness.

Heroism is about ordinary people doing extraordinary things. Motivation is about persuading ordinary people that they can achieve above ordinary things. Leadership is not just about winning – it's about keeping the team together. Shackleton was perhaps the greatest leader in the history of exploration, his polar expedition one of the greatest stories of motivation and human achievement…yet his expedition failed. Yet he is revered precisely because he valued human life and the sanctity of the team above all.

It's time to let go. You have done all that has been expected of you – and more. You trained as a team; you have survived as a team; you must now end this as a team. You can get off this boat now, proud of what you have done and knowing that everyone who has supported you in this endeavour believes that you have demonstrated the incredible ability of human beings to achieve incredible things. You have lived an incredible story – it's now time to end this chapter and start telling people how you did it. I know how disappointed you must feel – but you should not. You should be proud. And I am immensely proud to have been associated with this great adventure. As your major sponsor, but more important as I hope a lifelong friend, it's time to let go, to move on. It's time to come home".

Huddled in our survival cabin, with the roar of the storm outside, and the jarring and juddering as our boat scudded across the wave tops like a drunken driver, this email saved us from despondency. What Scipio wrote was true. We had fought and played hard as a team for over a year, focusing on one goal, supporting one another through those painful training sessions, grappling with new skills and learning all the time. We had achieved so much. Feeling sorry for ourselves was not our style and would do us no good. We had to adjust, set new goals and work to achieve them.

We agreed on the following steps:
  Step 1 – Patch up the boat and survive the storm as best we could.
  Step 2 – Use the technology we had on board as much as possible to help HMAS Newcastle to find us.
  Step 3 – Get home safely to join our friends and our families.
  Step 4 – Evaluate our experience and take time to reflect on our plans for the future.
  Step 5 – Continue to raise as much money as possible for SPARKS.

These were goals that we could give our hearts and souls to.

We had long periods of silence – strange for us – followed by discussions on how best to protect ourselves in the storm. We spoke of the positioning of the life raft, how we would get out if the boat went upside down, what equipment we would take with us and how long we thought the storm would last. Our conversations were short as we still found it difficult to talk of anything other than our progress across the ocean.

Now we had to survive for three or four days and hope HMAS Newcastle would find us bobbing about in the ocean. Rick had said he would get the ship's satellite telephone numbers so that we could make contact. Rob took charge of this as I was groggy and sick.

*

CHAPTER NINE
WAITING

*

*"When you get to the end of your rope,
tie a knot and hang on"*
Franklin D. Roosevelt

Day 46
Day one of the rest of our lives began with the shrill ring tone of our satellite telephone. I looked at my watch - 0415 hours - and fumbled in the pitching darkness for the waterproof bag beside my head. When I grabbed the phone it stopped ringing. There was no caller ID. Suddenly I felt sick and scrambled for the hatch. The bile rose in my throat and I just manage to get my head out before vomiting. It all went straight into the well, mixing with the slopping seawater.

"Are you alright?" Rob mumbled from the depths of his puffer jacket.

"It'll pass. Don't worry, go back to sleep", I replied unenthusiastically.

I was filled with abject misery as I hung out of the hatch, chilled by pelting rain and sea-spray and awaiting my next bout of nausea. Then a wave hit the side of the boat and diluted vomit splashed over my face as I smashed the side of my head on the hatch's metal rim. At least it was the good side. I didn't want to be bashed about outside or to keep throwing up inside. I wedged my head against the hatch opening and braced my legs and feet against the far wall of the cabin. At least now I could vomit in peace. After an hour of this, I felt exhausted but better, and returned to the sanctuary of the cabin and Rob's snoring.

I was freezing and wrapped myself in damp clothing before trying to sleep. Sheltering under my Norwegian shirt I could smell my vomit, which had become encrusted on my face with sea salt. I can cope with a lot of physical hardship but lying down like a wino in a ditch was too much for me. I cursed aloud, got up and grabbed my water bottle with a half-pint of the fresh stuff. Using a dirty t-shirt as a flannel, I washed my face and immediately felt fresher. It might be precious drinking water but it was a worthy cause. My ablutions were completed with a squeeze of toothpaste and I felt almost human.

The first traces of dawn appeared faintly on the Eastern horizon. My thoughts turned to home. I knew my family would be distressed and I felt guilty about putting them through something that was beyond their control. At least I had managed to speak to Buffy. I knew she would contact everyone, especially family members, and put a brave face on things. Whenever I spoke to her, I felt an overwhelming sense of her support.

I wondered how my father was taking the news. His wartime experiences had left him an optimist and a graduate of the stiff upper lip school. But dad had become more conscious of our shaky mortal hold on this world when mum passed away - they had been together since 1944. He wouldn't show it but he would be worried sick. I resolved to call him when our situation looked better.

Back home Buffy wrote:
"The story of Mike and Rob's plight slowly became public property. The local radio station phoned me and then a local BBC TV crew came to interview us at home. The children thought it was great - a satellite van outside our house and the opportunity to look inside to see how things worked. Michael Collier from the BBC was wonderful, full of compassion and understanding. At this stage I didn't see the press as an intrusion and I was happy to give them news. Michael noticed the candles flickering in front of a large plate that my friend Vanessa had painted intuitively for me, showing a lady looking out to sea. My crystal book lay open beside it, with a photo of Mike and Rob. Michael asked me about this and I explained a little about how, with the help of my friends, I was consciously projecting healing energies to Mike and Rob. But I was very wary, not wanting to appear a crank on television – I knew it wouldn't help Mike's cause.

My faith in Mike's ultimate safety was strong but I was on an emotional roller coaster. He called quite often. Sometimes he knew that he was calling me but other times he would fade away mid-sentence, leaving me to listen to the whooshing of the distant ocean.

I had to keep things together for the family. I was afraid that if I let my feelings out I wouldn't know how to control them. One night as I began to relax into sleep, the phone rang. I rushed to it, thinking it might be Mike, lost in his own time. But it was an Australian radio station wanting an interview for their early morning listeners. My sense of humour prevailed and I agreed. I explained how well prepared Mike and Rob had been and said that even if one of them had lost an arm they could have coped: they had the medical expertise for such an emergency. The problem with a head injury was that you often didn't know how bad it was until the worst happened - and that could be weeks later if there was a blood clot on the brain. The interview ended and I tried to drift off, only to be shaken by another call. Not Mike this time either. It was someone else in Australia wanting an interview. 'Sorry, I am too tired', I said this time".

The light penetrated the hatch window and I propped myself on my elbows for the discouraging view: grey clouds scudding from the South and a churned-up sea that mirrored my stomach. Out on deck a set of oars had become loose in the night and, although still attached to the retaining ropes, they sloshed about. One was clearly broken. The front navigation light mast was bent at the base - testimony to the continued ferocity of the waves. Rob would have to go out and make some running repairs. I closed my eyes to the chaos. Breakfast soon. I wondered if I could hold any of it down. But I wasn't thirsty or hungry. My head felt as though it was being slowly squeezed in a giant vice. I started to become unaware of the cold inside the cabin and the noise outside.

"Come on mate, we have been through a lot together you and I. It could be worse, a lot worse".

I groggily sensed that I was slipping in and out of consciousness and talking to myself.

"What's that mate?"

I opened my eyes to peer at Rob who was looking intently at me. My left eye fluttered again and my nose felt blocked with congealed blood.

"Look, I'm sorry mate. This is a shit position for you to be in and it's entirely my fault".

The words had burbled out, and I knew I was talking garbage. Hell no, this wasn't my fault, or anyone's. It had happened to me, but it could just as easily have been Rob getting whacked by a rogue wave. It was the roll of the dice.

But the tables were turned. Before *that* wave, I had felt in charge, calling the shots and playing the father figure. Now Rob had stepped up to the plate to look after me, himself and the boat. For the first time since we began, I could not fully participate. It felt like I had become baggage. I felt terribly powerless.

"Hey, don't you start talking like that. It could have been me and well you know it. We have got a long way to go yet and I need you to help me. Let's get some breakfast on the go".

It was typical of Rob to put things into perspective and this boosted my faltering morale.

Then the phone rang again and I passed it straight to Rob. It was Lee calling from America. He had seen the breaking news about us on CNN and he gave Rob his weather forecast for the next three days. I knew it was bad news when Rob just scribbled some notes instead of repeating everything as he usually did.

I quizzed him after he cut the connection. Over the next 48 hours the Southerlies would increase, with gusts of up to 55 knots meaning an even higher sea state with swells reaching 15 metres. With our impotent sea anchor we could expect to be driven northwards at 3-5 knots an hour - 100 miles or more in 24 hours. With the Southerlies blowing straight out across the Southern Ocean from Antarctica the night-time air temperature might be as low as eight degrees.

"This is going to be a rough ride", said Rob.

I lay down, imagining what the weather might do to our little boat. With the big sea anchor I had come to think that we could cope with almost anything. But I had no confidence in the pathetic effort that had replaced it.

Rob opened the inside compartment holding our cooker to prepare breakfast. Reaching for the water bottle he saw that we had only half a pint left. Outside, the two containers in the well were empty. Over the past 24 hours of trauma we had forgotten to pump any water.

"Shit", he said and disappeared out on deck. I heard him swearing and grunting as he tried to get one of the ballast containers out through the hole on

Wild Waters in the Roar

the deck. I didn't feel like going out to help and so I took the handheld water maker and started pumping. It was an agonizingly slow process, reflecting our pathetic situation.

Twenty minutes later Rob returned, soaked to the skin but proudly clutching a two galleon container. I stopped pumping while he poured more water into my bottle. The doctors back home had told him to keep me hydrated. I gulped a mouthful - only to spit it straight out.

"Christ Rob, what are you trying to do to me?"

He swigged some and copied me.

It was salt water! After all of Rob's hard work we discovered that the container had been contaminated by the sea. We had over twenty of these containers in the ballast hold. What if they were all contaminated? We could be in serious trouble. With the handheld machine we could only produce a measly pint an hour if we were lucky. Our predicament seemed ever bleaker but we consoled ourselves by munching quietly on a cold boil-in-the-bag chicken casserole. I had zero appetite but knew I needed the fluids. Rob pumped the handheld for half an hour and selflessly handed all the fresh water to me.

The satellite phone broke the silence again. It was Commander Steve Hughes, the Executive Officer on HMAS Newcastle. Just knowing that we had this link raised our spirits skywards. Commander Hughes spoke enthusiastically to Rob about his rescue plan. Despite the bad weather, his ship was steaming towards us at 20 knots and he hoped to reach us early on Thursday morning. They agreed to speak every four hours for updates on the weather and on our position. HMAS Newcastle would keep adjusting its course to cater for our northward drift.

I spoke briefly to Steve before he handed me over to the ship's doctor, Lieutenant Sue Sharpe. She reiterated that I had to drink plenty of water. As I described our plight, I could hear her tell Steve in the background that they needed to get a move on.

But - despite my head, despite the weather, despite the drought, despite everything -we felt hopeful. We just had to ride out the storms for another 72 hours.

★

Day 47

At midnight Rob went out to check our position, ready for a call from HMAS Newcastle at 0200 hrs. The GPS showed that we had continued to drift relentlessly northwards. The reserve sea anchor was useless. We had less cause to worry about our direction now that our goal was simply to survive. Back in the cabin, Rob looked at me desperately. In his eyes and body language I read his thoughts before he spoke.

"What if you felt better tomorrow…?" he mumbled.

Silence.

I tried to think carefully.

"Yeah, what if I did, what then?"

"Well, if you felt ok, we could tell the Newcastle that we didn't need them anymore, that we were going on. They'd understand, wouldn't they?"

I thought some more. I **was** feeling a bit better. I wasn't vomiting as often, and I hadn't passed out for at least 12 hours. Maybe I was turning the corner, maybe… Dammit … he was right. We could tell HMAS Newcastle that we no longer needed their assistance, I was ok, we could sort out the water maker, patch up the hole in the bow and the weather would calm down. Yes, we could carry on and fulfil our dream by completing this journey. After all, what would happen if we suddenly 'lost' our satellite phone over the side and the Argos tracking beacon malfunctioned? We would be on our own. No one could track us or contact us, and we'd just get on with it.

These crazy thoughts whisked around in my brain for seconds as the devil invaded my consciousness and taunted me in his cruel game of advocate. Then I firmly banished him. I remembered a conversation with Rob's father at Heathrow just before we flew out to Australia. I had promised to look after his son. I couldn't break my word. I also imagined Buffy's response. It was inconceivable that we could be so reckless.

"No Rob, stop being a prat", I said.

"We have finished this journey and we're playing extra time, waiting for the ref to blow the whistle so we can get off the pitch".

Rob looked at me sympathetically. At that moment we probably felt closer than ever.

With military precision, Commander Hughes rang at 0200 hours and briefed Rob on the poor weather. Even a huge warship is affected by the power of the ocean and they had been forced to slow down and stray from their path towards us to avoid the centre of the storm. Now their estimated time of arrival was Thursday lunchtime rather than dawn.

The prospect of even a six hour delay was unsettling. I studied the chart and plotted the positions of TRANSVenture and HMAS Newcastle. The distance between us looked vast. Negative thoughts filled my head. What if they didn't get here in time? What if they missed us? What if they had a problem?

"What's that noise?" Rob's question jolted me.

I strained my ears but could hear only the wind and the waves outside the cabin.

"There it is again".

Then I heard it - a low groaning from the plywood behind Rob's head at the back of the cabin.

We cleared away some sweaty t-shirts that were hanging up and I was relieved not to see any spurting water. I was carefully inspecting the wood when a wave bashed the side of the boat and shoved me forwards. Incredibly, I smashed my face once more and my nose started bleeding again.

Then I noticed that the stern panel was flexing against the side panel. It was bending to the pressure of the sea. My mind was flooded with a vision of the panel detaching and the ocean roaring in. Rob and I watched in fascination as it moved a couple of centimetres every half minute. It was as though we were part of the ocean's breath.

I realised that we could no longer rely on the solidity of our boat. This faith had sustained me through the worst of storms but now we were clearly at the mercy of the ocean. Would it choose to play one last card against us?

We had some spare marine plywood board and fibre glass but it was for minor repairs, not major surgery. We decided just to hide the flexing again with our smelly t-shirts. Out of sight, out of mind. Rob would have to pump up the volume on his boogie box to drown out the sound.

Back in the UK the pressure on Buffy was mounting:

"Life was hectic as newspapers, radio stations and TV channels became absorbed by the rescue attempt. Was there really no other worthy news in the world? I was trapped by the media, with three satellite vans and a clutter of cars blocking the way out of my home. Our friends rallied round by doing the school runs and agreeing to look after the children when I left for Australia. Stephie Watson, a dear friend of ours, fought her way

107

through the frenzied pack with £500 in an envelope. It was a godsend in the circumstances.

Journalists invaded my home and I couldn't move without having a microphone or camera shoved in my face for constant questions. I remember a man from Radio Five, more polite and reassuring than most, holding the microphone while someone hundreds of miles away interviewed me. The unseen face finally asked: "What will be your first words to Mike, when you meet up with him?" The chap smiled at me, as though he had read my mind ('what a stupid question to ask!') I burst into giggles and the interviewer closed with the comment that it was clearly going to be an emotional reunion.

The film crews all wanted to be there to capture the Mike's call saying that they were safely on board HMAS Newcastle. But I'd had enough and asked everyone to leave the house. However, I couldn't answer the phone without cameras filming me from outside and my phone chat with a friend was broadcast by one channel as showing me receiving the call from Mike.

Our family learnt a lot about how the media works and how some TV news reports are contrived. It was disturbing to witness a TV crew's excitement when they heard of a tragedy while I was being interviewed. They seemed almost disappointed to learn that the explosion in Paris had been caused by gas, not terrorists.

I was even asked to appear on breakfast television and the caller, who was trying to fill a spot, sounded unimpressed when I refused. 'We will send a car, and you can bring the kids as well' she pleaded. 'Thank you, but no thanks' I said".

☆

Day 48

The light stole into the forbidding night, turning the black to grey and unveiling a familiar landscape of water touching the sky and in eternal flux, like the journeys of our lives.

It also revealed a well full of salt water. Rob grabbed a bucket and started bailing out. It was time that I said 'good morning' to the world and I ventured on deck for the first time since I'd put out the spare sea anchor three days before.

Wild Waters in the Roar

Our treasured TRANSVenture was in a sorry state. The oar gates, until recently ever primed and ready for use, sat stiff in their mounts, crusted in salt. The deck was stained with black stripes from the grease that oiled our rowing tracks and had become mixed with sea water. The plastic compartment where the mechanical water maker had once quietly buzzed was badly cracked. The GPS mounted on the bulkhead no longer beamed out our position. Instead its diminished glow barely revealed any data as our batteries struggled for power. One of the solar panels had become partly detached from the roof, explaining the vibrating kerfuffle that accompanied each crash of waves over the boat. But our purple wind direction flag, tattered and torn, still fluttered defiantly above our heads in the fresh breeze.

We sat on deck, harnessed to the jackstay lines, munching on energy bars and nuts for breakfast. The wind whipped up the sea just enough to blow spray into our faces as we discussed the arrival of HMAS Newcastle. I tried to envisage the rescue: would they lift us by helicopter or send a small inflatable to pluck us out? I was worried about our boat. We had borrowed this trusty beauty and I shuddered at the thought that we might not be able to return her in a reasonable shape to her rightful owner. Thankfully Rob and Steve had talked about rescuing TRANSVenture, although of course saving our lives was the priority.

The day took on a painful torpor. Everything – even making a brew or a meal - happened in slow motion. The hopeful urgency of our rowing days had given way to lethargy. Before the crisis, we had handed over at the end of each rowing session with an iron discipline: neither of us would stop until the other was firmly on his seat and powering the oars. Every minute had counted then but now they seemed like hours. How many times, on the ergo rowing machine back home, had we chased the seconds vanishing on the countdown clock as we fought for new personal bests? Now the time wouldn't go fast enough.

In the afternoon we were driven back inside the cabin by turbulent seas. We had pumped nearly six pints of water and I enjoyed a large drink with cold meatballs in tomato sauce for supper.

The outdoor GPS dials were failing to register because there was no sun to generate electricity. I dug out my handheld GPS stored in our emergency grab bag, and plotted our position ready for the next call from HMAS Newcastle.

Then I called Buffy. She said she was flying out to Perth to meet us when we docked sometime next week. This cheered me up immeasurably. I also spoke briefly to the children who sounded a bit stressed. It was hard for them to ignore the media coverage with reporters making the most of the dangers we faced. I tried to reassure them that it wasn't all that bad but, when I put the phone down, I broke down and gave way to tears for the first time. I was putting my dearest ones through hell and I felt guilty and inadequate. I wanted to be home right now, holding them all in my arms, laughing and crying with them.

It was another long and painful night. I slipped into a version of a recurring nightmare. The rogue wave had grabbed me again but I wasn't secured by the safety harness and landed in the wild waters. I swam manically, not quite managing to keep up with the boat. At least I didn't drown.

★

Day 49

I apologised to Rob for disturbing him and shut my eyes to a new horror movie.

Rob and I were entangled in lines under our upturned boat. I struggled to deploy the life raft, but it started sinking into the depths and I desperately tried to grab the rope attached to it. Three huge sharks came into view. A boat drew up nearby and a man in a full immersion suit waved a satellite phone at me. I couldn't make out what he was shouting as the sound was muffled beneath the waves. A shark brushed past me, its sandpaper skin rasping against the backs of my legs. I opened my mouth to scream and swallowed seawater. I looked across at Rob and saw a darkened silhouette fending off another shark. Everything started to go dark…

It wasn't my best night's sleep but at least the HMAS Newcastle was due to reach us tomorrow evening. Commander Hughes explained that they would use their inflatable craft. It would be difficult in the dark and everything depended on the state of the sea. We had drifted 250 miles north of the point where we had abandoned the row. At this rate we would bump into Sri Lanka before they arrived.

For Buffy there was much to do:

"I had to sort things out for my departure. Stuart Ross from Betfair was an absolute darling and he arranged for me to stay with some of his friends in

Perth. This was wonderful news as it meant that the press would be unable to find me. I had agreed to just one interview when I reached Australia. Exhausted but relieved, I was driven to Heathrow by Geoff who lifted my mood with a few jokes about being chased by the paparazzi. My hardest task was to stay awake until I got on the plane".

Wednesday seemed like the longest day of my life. There was nothing to do except lie in the coffin being hurled from side to side and watch the clock. Our small radio had packed in and so we couldn't even listen to the repeat of 'The Archers' on the World Service.

As the dreary grey light turned black, I realised that this would probably be our last night on board our little boat. I felt sad and also apprehensive about the encroaching 'real world'.

CHAPTER TEN
RESCUE

*

'The worst thing you can possibly do is worry about what you could have done'
Lichtenberg

Day 50

Thursday morning at last. I couldn't help fretting that HMAS Newcastle wouldn't be able to pick us up in these rough seas. Rob and I prepared for the worst by moving food stocks from the deck containers into the cabin. Rick called to say that the storm should have passed us by midnight but, looking out of the hatch window, I couldn't share his optimism. Then the phone rang again with the news that HMAS Newcastle was less than 100 nautical miles away. They were sending a helicopter out to check on us. We started to feel excited until our attention was seized by a huge diversion - a 107,215 tonne oil bulk carrier, the Stena Confidence, powering towards us.

She was the first man-made object beyond our boat that we had seen for about forty days, and a vast mass of grey and black. As she drew closer we made out her white painted bridge, several storeys above sea level, and sailors like ants on the top deck.

Rob talked to the skipper who didn't speak much English but offered to put us on his lee side to shelter us from the elements until the Newcastle arrived. It turned out that the Bermuda-registered tanker was on her maiden voyage. There's an old maritime superstition that, if a ship and its crew rescue imperilled folk on their first trip, they will have eternal good luck. With this in mind, the skipper was determined to help us somehow. But he underestimated the challenge of tightly manoeuvring a quarter-mile ship in heavy seas and, before we knew it, she was just 50 metres away and we were in danger of being crushed. We anxiously watched the battle of titans as the skipper tried to reverse his craft against the might of the ocean swell. The seas crashed furiously against his stern and smoke belched from the engine funnels as he persisted for twenty minutes before bowing to the superior force of nature.

He radioed to say that he couldn't safely align his tanker beside our tiny craft. Thank goodness!

"Would you mind moving away to the South?" Rob had earlier asked him before I grabbed the radio and firmly said: "Please leave the area before you sink us".

But the skipper made one last try to help us. Would we like him to drop us some coffee, water and cigarettes? We were sorely tempted until we realised that he planned to drop them from a height of fifty foot! And so, after bidding us good luck, the Stena Confidence left our world and we settled back in the cabin to prepare for the arrival of HMAS Newcastle.

Through the day Rob kept the Executive Officer Steve Hughes fully briefed on our location. He also gave him full details on TRANSVenture - her weight, length, potential strop points for lifting, and the extent of her damage. This wasn't a search and rescue operation – at no time did we activate a 'mayday' call or deploy our EPIRBs. Everything was carefully planned.

6 hours before rescue, Tiger 76 buzzes us

Just before last light we heard the unmistakeable wocker-wocker of helicopter blades. I opened the small rear cabin hatch but saw only the towering swell obscuring most of the fading sky. Then a tiny object appeared. Seahawk helicopter Tiger 76 was approaching from the north and the pilot called us on our handheld VHF radio. Would we go on deck so that their official press officer could take some photographs? We weren't expecting this and Rob tried to say no but was told that there was huge interest from the British and Australian media who wanted a shot of us 'looking hard' with stiff upper lips! We duly did as we were asked while the Seahawk buzzed around us for twenty minutes. It was strange to watch this flying technology after our weeks away from civilisation. I could make out the pilot's face and wondered what he was thinking. For a moment I wished we could climb on board rather than wait several more hours for the ship. But Tiger 76 provided a huge boost to our morale. We knew that we would be rescued soon. The bad news was that it would happen in pitch darkness in violent seas. The pilot explained that his skipper had decided it was worth a try since the weather would only get worse – the sooner, the better.

☆

Day 51

Just after midnight, and HMAS Newcastle was one nautical mile away. We'd agreed that Rob would fire a red flare once he saw her mast lights and the ship would respond with two white flares indicating that the RHIBs (Rigid Hard Inflatable Boats) were on their way. He pulled the ignition but, instead of the flare deploying in a graceful skyward arc, it stayed in its casing, heating towards 230 degrees Celsius. With a cry of '"bugger" Rob threw it into the water to sink gently to the depths, leaving an eerie trail of red phosphorus. Thinking that he was messing about, I grabbed another flare and pulled the pin for the same result – a burnt hand. We creased up laughing as we imagined what the Newcastle crew, viewing us through night vision devices, must be thinking of these mad Poms.

But third time lucky - with a whoosh the flare popped into the night sky, illuminating us with shadowy red light. Within minutes we heard the RHIBs' propeller screws churning through the swell towards us. Out of the darkness came a strong white light and the first RHIB was upon us. It was a big, black, inflatable beast - almost the same size as our boat and with powerful dual engines. It hit the crest of a wave and was airborne before crashing down impressively. As it passed our stern to turn and head back into the waves beside us, I glimpsed six people; all dressed in immersion suits and with head torches and life preservers. The master driver stood at the wheel. In his helmet and goggles he looked like an intimidating Darth Vader. Then the RHIB rode up on a wave and crashed onto our forward deck, making us fall over before it slipped back down. Swiftly lines were tied to our aft and stern while the second RHIB drew up and did the same on our other side. We were securely pinned between these beasts. A man jumped onto our deck and - through the cacophony of wind, sea and diesel engine - yelled at us to board his RHIB.

"Strewth mate, where's the rest of it?" he drawled, gazing around our beloved boat.

"Jesus, what's that smell!" he joked as we got closer.

Clutching my grab bag I reached out towards the bobbing RHIB and two shovel- sized hands unceremoniously pulled me aboard. I sat on a torpedo shaped seat and was strapped onto the handrail. Rob quickly followed and suddenly we were racing off into the darkness. It felt weird, pounding through the swell on a different boat to the one we had lived on for more than six weeks. The second RHIB stayed to take ours under tow to the Newcastle. I looked back at her, bobbing beyond our control, and felt sad and concerned for her safety. Sounds silly I know, but she had been our home for a long time and we had abandoned her. Our small vessel had preserved us despite everything that Mother Nature had thrown at us. I prayed that the crew could save her. If not, they would have to sink her at sea so that she did not endanger other vessels.

The ship's doctor was behind me, shouting questions in my ear about whether I was fit enough to climb a ladder. I felt bloody awful but just nodded and gave her the thumbs up. She kept shining a torch at me. I remember big grey waves crashing everywhere and her worried face.

The journey took about ten minutes but it seemed like hours. We smashed through formidable waves: climbing upwards, the engine screws biting hard, breaking over the top and accelerating down the front into the troughs. Then the engines changed note as they fought to bite the water. The frantic pace and buffeting was simultaneously exhilarating and terrifying. All around unintelligible commands were shouted as we careered along, constantly sprayed by the ocean. I wondered if we were really in control, so unnatural seemed our skidding across the water. As I looked back at Darth Vader, he seemed to be laughing. Was he mad, or just enjoying our fear? The truth was probably that he didn't often have such fun, surfing the waves at breakneck speeds.

The smudgy outline of HMAS Newcastle appeared on our horizon. She was clearly at 'battle stations' as the only visible lights were high up on the mast while the bridge was bathed in a soft red glow.

This was the moment of truth. Rob and I were apprehensive about the reception we would get. We had talked about this for the past five days. We weren't looking for sympathy but we hoped that they would understand what we'd tried to achieve and not treat us like a couple of nutters. From Rob's conversations with the Executive Officer we knew that our rescue team were missing a rugby international for their trouble. We understood only too well what a sacrifice this was!

As we approached the port side of the frigate I saw the rope ladder dangling down. Our RHIB started to jockey alongside it - no mean feat of skill by Darth Vader who delicately inched us towards the ship. I reached out for the side of the gun-metal coloured hull and realised that we were pitching about four metres up and down in the swell. Timing would be crucial in getting onto the ladder. It would be an act of faith in the bosun. If he misjudged the swell we could fall and be crushed between RHIB and warship. The doctor went first, casually stepping onto the bottom rung and scurrying upwards. I was amazed there was no safety rope thrown down beside the ladder, but I didn't want to appear a wimp by asking for one.

"Bloody hell boys, we got a pack of teeth on our tail!"

Darth Vader had spied some big fish below us. Or so he said. I knew then that I was going to get on that ladder and not take an early bath. Off went Rob, as if on a stroll in the park. Me next. I remember thinking: please God, make sure my arms are strong enough for this. "Go!" shouted Darth Vader and I stepped into the air, grasping the ladder like a demon. Then I realised that the giant warship was almost impervious to the swell and, within thirty seconds, I was being pulled onto the deck to be greeted by Captain Gerry Christian and his Executive Officer Steve Hughes. It was 0210 hours. The whole operation from the moment we fired the flares had taken just thirty-five minutes.

So, what of our rescue ship, HMAS Newcastle?

She is a multi-role warship capable of anti submarine, air defence, surveillance and reconnaissance duties. She displaces 4100 tonnes, is 138 metres long, can travel at more than 30 knots and, with her helicopter crews, has a ship's complement of around 210 personnel. The Commanding Officer, Capt Gerry Christian is the great-great-great-great grandson of the famous Fletcher Christian who led the mutiny on the British navy ship HMS Bounty in 1789!

The following account in 'Navy News', the official newspaper of the Royal Australian Navy, modestly underlines the crew's consummate professionalism.

"... HMAS Newcastle (Capt Gerry Christian) headed deep into the Indian Ocean to rescue a Briton who suffered serious injuries when he was thrown head first into the gunwale of the 7 metre plywood boat he and a friend were trying to row from Australia to an island off Africa.

"Rescued were 45-year-old Mike Noel-Smith and Rob Abernethy, 31. The two Britons set off from Carnarvon earlier this year to row to Reunion Island off Africa in a bid to raise money for a children's charity.

"The emergency, which spanned ten days, saw Newcastle proceed to a position 1400 nautical miles WNW of Exmouth. The pair were 45 days into the row deep into the Indian Ocean south west of the Cocos Islands when their craft was hit by high waves and one rogue wave during a significant storm. Damage to Mike Noel-Smith was also accompanied by damage to their rudder and bow of their boat. The rogue wave had hurled Mike Noel-Smith face first into the gunwale, where he suffered severe concussion a broken nose, possible detached right eye retina and other injuries.

"By Monday June 2 his condition had deteriorated and Rob Abernethy sought medical advice using sat phone. The response from the medical team in the UK was he needed medical help as soon as possible.

"The Rescue Coordination Centre in Canberra determined that HMAS Newcastle was the nearest ship with a doctor on board and she was tasked to assist the rowers. At the time she was south of Christmas Island en route to a port visit at Bunbury.

"Capt Gerry Christian ordered a turn to starboard and at 22 knots the warship headed west with 1125 nm to steam. Shortly before sunset on June 5 Newcastle launched her Seahawk helicopter, 'Tiger 76' to search for the boat. The aviators found the craft and reported her position by radio. Newcastle quickly closed and arrived 1 nm from the boat after dark.

"In marginal conditions safe to operate in, she launched her RHIBs with medical personnel on board and they went across to the stricken boat. The Britons were transferred to Newcastle's medical facility...

"Capt Gerry Christian praised his crew for their professionalism and slick drills to make the whole operation smooth and workmanlike. He also added that the rowers had contributed enormously to the operation with use of sat phone, tracking beacon and radar reflector to assist in the accurate location of their vessel. HMAS Newcastle will now steam to Fremantle and is expected to arrive sometime around 10 June".

There was little pitch and roll on the Newcastle and, unaccustomed to the stability, Rob and I staggered around like drunkards. I was whisked down to the medical sick bay where navy doctor Lieutenant Sue Sharpe put me though a series of tests. She diagnosed concussion and serious dehydration but said there was only minor damage to my nose. She was concerned about any internal damage to my head – when we docked I would have to go straight to Perth General Hospital for a scan. I was worried only about my flickering right eye but Sue reassured me that this would pass.

I charged up our satellite phone and made lots of calls. It was great to be able to reassure everyone, especially my father who had no internet access for instant news and had been very worried.

Meanwhile Rob briefed the senior officers and then sneaked off for a shave and shower. When I saw him in the sick bay he literally smelt of roses. Then it was my turn and by God did I need it. Having hot water cascading down my body was sheer bliss and I wallowed in the bubbles and steam for ages.

Then we tucked into pie and chips - a welcome feast especially since we had both lost a couple of stones.

We were to sleep in the medical bay, and it was heavenly slipping between clean sheets after the smelly rigor of our coffin floor. The staff gave us sleeping pills but, sure enough, every two hours I was awake expecting to get out and row.

Rob wandered off to the all-ranks mess deck where he discovered an ice cream machine. He returned with the two biggest ice creams I have ever seen, complete with chocolate flakes, and we sat on our bunks like Cheshire cats. I was confined to the medical ward for forty-eight hours and so Rob became my not entirely willing ice cream runner.

The crew of HMAS Newcastle present us with a cheque for our charity – in return we give them one of our oars

Steve Hughes came down with the fantastic news that they had saved TRANSVenture. He showed us an infrared recording of the recovery operation which involved divers placing large strops around her hull that were attached to a crane so that they could winch her aboard. Halfway up however, one of the strops was displaced and TRANSVenture would have plunged back down but for the quick work of the crane operator.

We couldn't have had a warmer reception - we were bathed in hospitality. Everyone we met wanted to talk to us. We were given a full ship's tour and, as ex-military men, a briefing on pretty much everything that happens aboard a warship. We were royally entertained by all the ratings as we went round giving presentations on our adventures.

On our last day before docking into Fremantle, we were presented with a thousand Australian dollars for our SPARKS charity. In turn we presented the ship with a broken oar. It was pretty much all we had to give them but it was received with three loud cheers from the whole ship's company.

Our final task at sea was to prepare for the media. It was agreed that Rob and Captain Christian would make prepared statements while I slipped off to hospital. At a rehearsal in the officer's ward room Rob practised fielding a mix of friendly and hostile questions. I'm sure he was nervous but he still exuded his usual confidence.

As the sun came up on the ninth of June, I went on deck to view the still blurred coastline of Australia and the small island of Rottnest, nestling off Fremantle. The sea slept as the bow of the warship cut through her like soft butter. Seabirds hovered above, looking for titbits. It was idyllic.

I knew that Buffy was close, waiting for me on the quayside. I hoped the press was not pestering her too much.

Then, as the warship conducted it docking manoeuvres, I spotted her beside the milling reporters and TV crews, looking up and waving. The captain had kindly allowed her to come aboard so that we could share some private moments.

"Hello darling, like the beard!" were her first words.

Tears and hugs gave way to smiles and laughter, as we embraced in a swell of emotions. Buffy held me so tightly that I thought she would crush my ribs and, when she was taken on a quick tour of the boat, she would not let go of my hand – as if I might suddenly vanish.

Then we said goodbye to our Australian friends and stepped onto dry land where we pushed through the throng to get to our ambulance. With cameras prying through the windows, I looked out to see Rob and Captain Christian walking down to face the press.

This is what Rob said:

"Good morning Ladies and Gentlemen. My name is Rob Abernethy. On behalf of myself and my colleague, Mike Noel-Smith, I would like to issue the following brief statement before handing over to the Commanding Officer of HMAS Newcastle.

First and foremost I would like to convey our eternal thanks to the Officers and Crew of HMAS Newcastle for coming to our assistance on 4th June 2003 and for the recovery of our ocean rowing boat, TRANSVenture. We have been extremely well looked after and Mike has received the best possible medical attention since our rescue some five days ago. These thanks I also echo on behalf of our family and friends in the United Kingdom, who have obviously followed events very closely. The excellent plan that the Captain and his staff formulated was conducted rapidly, professionally and safely throughout, allowing us to feel at all times extremely confident in its outcome.

"Our primary aim for conducting the row was to raise significant monies for the children's charity SPARKS. The specific benefactor of our fundraising activities is centred upon The University of Portsmouth, where the research team is helping to identify the causes and cures of meningitis, which has a high fatality rate in babies and young children. We feel passionately in raising funds for this excellent charity and will continue to do so upon our return to the United Kingdom.

"We are absolutely devastated that after a year and a half of extensive training, planning and analysis for this charity row that we are in this current situation. Throughout the past sixteen months we have liaised closely with the Sea Rescue Organisation of Western Australia, The Australian Bureau of Meteorology and many of the world's leading consultants, to ensure that we obtained the highest level of readiness to complete our mission. However, not even our paramedic training could have changed the outcome following the freak accident that led to us being in this position. Head injuries must be dealt with by specialist physicians and therefore the decision was made to abandon the row. We do believe that the fact that we had the most comprehensive equipment on board helped in some small way to the successful outcome of this operation.

"I would like to conclude this statement by reiterating both our thanks and that of our title sponsor Betfair; to the Officers and Crew of HMAS Newcastle and all the other agencies involved in this operation. Thank you".

*

CHAPTER ELEVEN
EPILOGUE

*

"Accept each part of the journey as it comes. Let each stretch of your path be what it needs to be".
Melody Beattie

*

The driver punctuated our short trip to Perth General Hospital with questions and then I had a full head and body scan. My biggest worry was my flickering eye. It turned out that the optical nerve was detached and this took weeks to recover. I also had intermittent headaches, lasting for months, though I was confident that that my faculties were intact.

I did several neurological tests: drawing a picture of a house, answering simple questions and walking in a line. The last was the hardest and I overheard Buffy giggling and reassuring a lady in the next cubicle that I wasn't drunk! The sight of a bearded man in an open-backed white gown lurching up the corridor must have been disturbing but, after 50 days at sea, I just couldn't walk straight.

I was surprised to learn that I had a broken ankle and recalled injuring it years before, playing football on the beach with the children.

After two hours I emerged into the Perth sunlight with an essentially clean bill of health and Lt Sue Sharpe's firm advice to 'take it easy'.

We collected our bags from Jonathan and Raynor Priest who had invited Buffy into their home and looked after her. The press were waiting for us at the Tradewinds Hotel in Fremantle and we agreed to two interviews: one with the BBC and an exclusive with the Daily Express about our reunion after all the drama and weeks apart. The fee would go to our charity SPARKS.

Reunited in Freemantle

Buffy gave me news that she had shielded me from during the voyage. I learnt that William had to sit an A level exam the morning he heard about my accident, that Buffy had been being pestered by insensitive journalists and that some of the reporting was hostile.

With Buffy's permission, I was delighted to shave off my beard. It made me look like an old badger and was extremely itchy.

Rob and I spent our last days in Australia ensuring the safe repatriation of TRANSVenture. My brother Denis spoke to Richard Large, who had been on the board of P&O, and he kindly arranged for the boat to be shipped home for free. Our weatherman Rick Friswell was another great help, driving our boat trailer 800 kilometres from his home in Carnarvon to Perth and helping us load TRANSVenture into her 40 foot container. Such wonderful people – they supported our venture all the way.

We flew into bright early morning sunshine at Heathrow on June 15th. As I walked down the cabin aisle, I realised that it would be more emotional seeing our families and friends now than when we left. Thankfully, airport staff provided a private room, away from the media pack, where I had a teary meeting with my children, William, Isabelle and Harry.

Then Rob and I went to face the hacks and their inevitable questions: 'Are you glad to be back?', 'Was it worth it?' and 'Don't you feel embarrassed you failed?' I will never understand why the negative dominates the positive in news reporting. After thirty minutes Denis came to our rescue, ushering us outside only to bump into a Sky TV crew with a satellite truck in the car park. I didn't want to be rude and, at last, it was time to return home to Hereford.

Rob was off to party in Fulham, full of tales of derring-do. As we said goodbye it dawned on me that we were going our separate ways for the first time in three months. It was a strange feeling. We had collaborated intimately, trusting each other with our lives, but now we would start making decisions independently again.

As Buffy had warned, the press coverage was mixed. Some of the criticism was ill-informed and some was downright rude. Jeremy Clarkson filled both categories, arguing that we had been a pointless burden to the Australian tax payer. He saw us as easy targets for another know-it-all column and a forthcoming book with disparaging comments about us and other adventurers.

Transventure unloads in Freemantle docks. The hole at the bow bears testimony to the forces of nature she had battled out on the Indian Ocean

Mike Noel-Smith

Mr Clarkson may not know of the ancient 'law of the sea' obliging ship's masters to rescue imperilled lives no matter what they are doing and where they are going. But I assume he has heard of own RNLI which has saved more than 100,000 people – some of them doing what Clarkson calls 'meaningless things'. We had been in an area of the Indian Ocean covered by Australia (under the terms of International Maritime Organisation) and the skipper of HMAS Newcastle, Captain Gerry Christian, was adamant that the cost of our rescue was minimal. He said it was a useful training opportunity using no more fuel than their normal fisheries protection duties. The crew was justly proud of the good PR gained by steaming to our aid.

We knew that our mission had substance. It helped to raise awareness of a disease that kills hundreds of children every year and funded research into a cure. I suspect it took more training, teamwork and spirit than Clarkson and co needed to race an Aston Martin DB9, Ferrari 612 Scaglietti and Mercedes-Benz SLR McLaren across Europe. It was certainly a less meaningless activity.

In contrast Sir Richard Branson praised our efforts, saying: "British history is full of great explorers, going right back to Cook and Darwin, (including) the ones who didn't succeed, like Shackleton of the Antarctic who is still a hero despite the fact that he tried and failed, and the same applies to these two."

Rob and I appeared on a couple of TV shows, which were fun opportunities to publicise our charity. On 'Ready, Steady, Cook' I prepared shark steak in pepper sauce with Paul Rankin, while Rob thrashed away with Lesley Waters cooking red snapper. I was delighted to win by three votes though, with four members of my family in the audience, I had an advantage!

TRANSVenture was in no fit state and we took part in 'They Think It's All Over' with a loaned rowing boat. We were the patsies in the 'feel the sports person' game, causing great audience amusement as David Seaman and Jonathan Ross clambered aboard blindfolded with comments like 'Wow, he's a big boy' and 'There's too much seaman in this boat'.

Creative Touch Films phoned to say that the first rough cut of the documentary was ready. How exciting! I got on the early train to Paddington train and settled down with a paper and coffee as the 125 sped through the countryside. Then, near Evesham, I heard a loud bang and the train jolted and bucked as the brakes were suddenly applied. Someone screamed

Wild Waters in the Roar

while plates and cups crashed in the buffet compartment. The prospect of derailing flashed through my mind. My God, I had survived the Indian Ocean and was going to die on a railway track. After half a mile the train slid to a halt.

Outside cows munched on the cud and ducks flew off from a nearby river. A guard came and explained we had just hit a minibus of fruit pickers. I consoled an elderly lady sitting in shock opposite me, with tears rolling down her cheeks.

Three hours later we rumbled into a small station to find the national press grabbing anyone they could think of. The Bishop and the MP for Hereford were obvious targets but I was recognised as the 'bloke from the ocean' and pursued to a waiting taxi. I politely said 'no', just wanting to get home. The cabbie told me that seven migrant workers had died in the accident.

Back home an ITV crew was waiting. As soon as they began comparing this tragedy to my ocean experiences, I told them to stop. Somewhere in Europe - I reminded them - mothers, wives, girlfriends, sons and daughters had lost loved ones on a dusty line in Gloucestershire. It was insensitive to make comparisons. That night Buffy lit a candle for the families of the poor souls who died going to pick fruit in an English orchard.

The Betfair marketing and media team arranged a flurry of charity fundraising and PR activities. At a black tie dinner in London, the former rugby international player Martin Bayfield raised a stunning £10,000 for SPARKS from 100 guests. My twin sister Bibi organised a function at her local church hall in Wimbledon, which was a great opportunity to meet her pals who had supported our venture. I had to give a 10 minute talk and felt quite nervous. But I was among friends. That night Rob's parents, Liz and Desmond, held a classical music evening in Devon and Rob took the floor. The two events raised another £7,500. We were still receiving cheques from all over the country. I wrote to everyone who donated to our cause. Without their support we could not have raised more than £80,000. We were delighted when, at the SPARKS Winter Ball, the Duchess of Kent saluted our efforts.

Rob and I gave a series of talks to businesses and schools, reliving our tales and trying to pass on some life lessons. We were asked all sorts of questions such as: 'How did you go to the toilet?', 'Did you ever argue?', 'Weren't you mad to do this?', 'What did your wife think?', 'Did you have any spiritual experiences?', and the inevitable 'Are you going to do it again?'

Back in Herefordshire it was sometimes hard to accept that our adventure was over. Everyday activities like collecting papers, buying petrol and strolling around the shops seemed trivial and odd. My fresh memories of the ocean's wilderness - where high winds froth the wave tops, the sun rises and falls majestically and the stars race through the heavens - made normal life seem boring.

I kept waking up in the small hours and going into the garden with two sleepy dogs, trying to identify stars and silently cursing the fuzziness of the night sky. During the day, my mind was flooded with flashbacks. I chuckled at people scurrying with scowls in the rain, dodging puddles and catching their clothes from the wind. We in the West have become perhaps too wary of the elements. We dash about and fail to appreciate our environment with its constant changes of weather and light. Our children are increasingly governed by social calendars, mobiles, the internet and electronic games. We are in danger of losing a precious skill: taking time to quietly reflect, to value Mother Earth and to be, instead of always doing. We must all live in our own ways but a relentless focus on material things is inevitably stressful and unfulfilling.

What did I learn from the voyage?

I set out with the attitude that I didn't like to lose at anything and wouldn't suffer fools gladly. I wasn't especially selfish, but I knew what I liked and what I didn't.

My sense of connection with a higher being had waned over the years, stirred only by infrequent visits to church, mainly for christenings, weddings and funerals. But I was taught by Carmelite priests and grew up quite a godly little chap. Inhaling the church atmosphere, gazing at the beautiful paintings and artefacts, singing in the school choir and learning to quote chunks of the Bible made me a 'believer'.

Joining the Army changed all that. I learnt that life is often unfair and men can be very cruel. I questioned whether God exists. How could he allow so much squalor, pain and suffering? Like many, I kept my doubts silent, seeing religion as a way of conveying good values to my children.

Yet the row turned into much more than an attempt to propel a one-ton boat for 3,500 miles. It became also a voyage of self-discovery and of spiritual re-awakening. As the days passed, the charitable dimension of our trip seemed increasingly important. The words of the Quaker preacher Stephan Grellat rang true:

"I expect to pass through this world but once. Any good, therefore, that I can do or any kindness I can show to any fellow creature, let me do it now. Let me not defer or neglect it for I shall not pass this way again".

On my return Buffy, who knows me better than anyone, said I was a more tolerant person.

But I am still essentially a man of action. My children have inherited my adventurous spirit, doing bungee jumps and climbing mountains. I support them in their 'wacky' activities because they supported me.

I try to live by these values:

- Do not compare – everyone is unique and comparisons are spurious.
- Trust your intuition - deep down you know when you are doing the right thing.
- Do what you love – rather than things that make you feel insecure.
- Don't worry about 'failure' - the only way to fail is to give up and stop learning.
- Don't rely on praise from others – how you see yourself is more important.
- Find collaborators and supporters - not people who are negative and drain your energy.
- Let go of irrational fear - life is too short. It is all right at times to be scared and to cry, but be sparing with this.

Was it worth it?

Let Theodore Roosevelt be my voice on this.

"It is not the critic who counts, not the man who points out how the strong man stumbled, or where the doer of deeds could have done better. The credit belongs to the man who is actually in the arena; whose face is marred by dust and sweat and blood; who strives valiantly; who errs and comes up short again and again; who knows the great enthusiasms, the great devotions, and spends himself in a worthy cause; who, at the best, knows in the end the triumph of high achievement; and who at worst, at least fails while daring greatly, so that his place shall never be with those cold and timid souls who know neither victory nor defeat".

Will I do it again?

Since our voyage there have been three more failed attempts to row unassisted across the Indian Ocean. No pair or team has officially succeeded. I cannot speak for Rob (who is newly married) but I know that, with my family's blessing, I will take up this challenge anew. My son, who as a strapping 23 year old having finished University will come with me. There is not a day that passes when I do not think about the Indian Ocean, the highs and lows. It has been mentioned that our journey was like the disaster that hit Apollo 13 – a successful failure. My memories cultivate a desire to return to the ever-changing ocean. Wildlife abounds in the most remote of wild waters and is always fascinating. The wind shifts instantly from calm to frenzy. Raindrops appear as big as tennis balls - can you imagine it? There is something magical about the ocean, feeling at one with her unspoilt beauty. This irresistible mistress draws you back again and again once you have tested her power, and you know that despite everything, you will always be at her mercy.

END

*

APPENDIX 1
GLOSSARY OF TERMS

*

Anti – Foul Paint – paint applied to any part of the boat that comes into contact with salt water. It prevents the build up of barnacles and growth. We used an eco-friendly solution which although was non harmful to life in the ocean did mean regular visits under the boat to stop a build up of our own eco-system hitching a ride!

Bow – The front end of the boat.

Broaching – Side onto the waves

Bioluminescence – what we call phosphorescence is due to light from a number of organisms, from microscopic marine life to larger deep water fish.

Breaking sea – The partial collapse of the crests of waves, less complete than in the case of breakers, but from the same cause; also known as White Horses.

Broach to – To slew around inadvertently broadside on to the sea, when running before it.

Confused sea – Waves meeting from different directions normally due to a sudden shift in the direction of the wind.

Continental shelf – A zone adjacent to a continent where shallow water gives way to deep oceanic waters. Normally between 100 – 350 miles from the lands end.

Ebb tide – a loose term applied both to the falling tide and to the outgoing tidal stream.

Eddy – A circular motion in water, existing in oceans as well as other water bodies.

Ergometer (Ergo) – Concept 2 type indoor rowing trainer

EPIRB – Emergency Position Indicating Radio Beacon. We had individual ones which we could strap to our ankles whilst rowing in heavy seas, plus a main one which we would carry in the liferaft if we had to deploy into that. The devices are used to alert would be rescuers if we were in need by accurately plotting us by a global satellite network.

Gunwale – the upper edge of the boat at deck level which support the oar gates

GPS – Global Positioning Satellite, instruments to assist with continuous world-wide position fixing. The system is fed by satellites 22,000 miles above the planet. It is operated by the United States Department of Defence, and is accurate down to 5m, although this is dependant on the number of satellites that the instruments can 'see'.

Inmarsat D+ – small satellite tracking device mounted in the bow compartment and contained in a sealed waterproof case. This tracked us every 6 hours.

Iridium Satellite Telephone – our voice contact with the outside world. We used a Motorola 6505 model which was also connected to our laptop computer to download weather data and to send/receive emails from around the world.

Jackstays – thin wire cable running both side of the deck in between the rowing rail, and used to secure our harnesses to during bad weather

Knot – The nautical unit of speed, i.e. 1 nautical mile (of 1852m) per hour. An example is 10 knots is equivalent to 12 miles per hour.

Lee side – The side of the ship or object which is away from the wind and therefore sheltered.

Nm – Nautical mile which measures 1852m on the international scale and is the unit of distance in nautical terms. 1 nm equal 1.15 miles.

Oar gate – the small plastic part at the end of the rigger that opens at the top. Once opened, the oar is placed in, the gate closed and screwed tight to prevent the oar slipping out.

Pitch – Angular motion of a ship in the fore-and-aft plane.

Port – The left hand side of the vessel when facing the bow (front end).

Rigger – the metal support attached on top of the gunwale that holds the oar gate.

Rhumb line – Any line on the Earth's surface which cuts all meridians at the same angle, i.e. a line of constant bearing.

SAR – Search and Rescue.

Scuppers – Holes just above the water line underneath the gunwales to allow the ocean to pour out.

Sea Anchor – Can also be called Para anchor, in general, regardless of conditions, parachute sea anchors keep the bow of the boat to wind, eliminating the chances of capsizing in heavy seas, and when deployed quickly and correctly the boat will become more stable even in 'big water'. Effectively it is a large parachute on the end of about 100m of rope that sinks below the water to a depth of anything around 5-10 metres.

SITREP – short for situation report, and is an old military term. We would try and send one of these reports every day for updating on our website.

SPARKS – SPort Aiding medical Research for KidS our designated charity.

Stag – Period of time, normally a 2 hour session when you are duty rowing, we tried to maintain a 2 hour on stag and 2 hour off regime.

Starboard – The right hand of the vessel when facing the bow (front end).

Stern – The rear end of the boat

TRANSVenture – short for The Rob Abernethy Noel Smith Venture and the name of our boat.

Well – Lower part of the deck, one outside the main cabin allows one to stand up, and one inside the cabin where we stored our gas cooker.

VHF – Abbreviation for Very High Frequency radio, the range of our handheld was approximately 10nm.

*

APPENDIX 2
FITNESS AND NUTRITION

*

Fitness in General

I am no expert on how to get fit to compete in a downhill ski event or to run a marathon, but both Rob and I went through a process to prepare our bodies for the ultimate endurance challenge of rowing across an ocean. We picked up loads of tips and ideas along the way, and I thought it would be useful to put them down in writing. Having said that, what was good for us, will not necessarily be good for others! Much will also depend on how much time is available to you and the proximity of a decent gym.

Much depends on how you want to approach physical training for such an arduous endurance 'sport' (I use the term loosely!) to row an ocean. To my mind, there are two schools – those that take it seriously and those who would rather not! Rob and I decided in moment one of deciding to row the Indian Ocean that we would do this seriously. We were massively helped by having a top British coach looking after us with Bill Black. He not only controlled our programmes but became a valuable motivator, mentor and friend in the long haul to prepare body, mind and soul. I would recommend anyone wanting to take the serious route to get a coach because it is invaluable to get feedback outside of a machine telling you how far you have gone in what time or how much weight you lifted. Personal and often critical communication by interacting with someone else is vital. Although Bill lived no-where near me, he telephoned just about everyday to see how things were going and to 'chivvy' me along. With Rob he had a big and fit guy from day 1, with me he had an older less fit guy to sort out. And sort me out he did!

The main thing that I learnt during our physical training regime was that slow and steady wins the race. Our programmes were based on steadily increasing the intensity of workouts in small amounts with plenty of rest period thrown in as well. This allowed for the challenge necessary for improvements without causing injury or 'burn out'. Too much too soon can over stress the body, limit the progress and increase the risk of injury.

Rowing requires a unique mix of power and endurance and, to a lesser degree technique, of both aerobic and anaerobic energy systems. Aerobic exercise is simply any exercise that uses large muscle groups and is the type of exercise that overloads the heart and lungs and causes them to work harder than when at rest. The types of exercises that we used in our training for the aerobic energy systems included cycling, running, swimming and power walking.

Anaerobic exercises burns more carbohydrates but can help increase metabolism to burn fat indirectly. The body is working so hard in these exercises that the demands for oxygen and fuel exceed the rate of supply and therefore the muscles have to rely on burning up stored reserves of fuel. When this happens, waste products accumulate, the chief one being lactic acid and the body's stored fuel ceases and reaches its threshold and stops – often painfully! We had to build the body to withstand long extended periods of work, followed by comparatively short periods of body rest before asking it to work again. Unlike a marathon, which after 3-4 hours of work the body can rest for days if necessary, we would be looking at maintaining a work rate of 12 hours physical effort each day for possibly 80 days! Of course, we never had that situation due to storms, but we had to prepare for the ideal scenario of rowing non stop to Reunion Island.

To compliment the normal exercise programme that Bill Black gave us on a monthly basis we also had core fitness training, strength, endurance and circuit training thrown into the pot. Bill was also at pains to tell us that the pre row training had been designed with a view to us 'peaking' somewhere near the 35 day mark so that we would still be physically capable well after the start of the voyage and not burnt out after a week on the high seas. A breakdown of the early days of training follows and what each 'discipline' means:

Core Stability Fitness

This refers to the level of control of the trunk during dynamic movement. It is balance, not strength that is important. There will be an increase of efficiency if the trunk is well controlled and in alignment. The limbs can then work optimally in swim, bike and run.

Exercises done daily:

2 x sets of 3 x 30 seconds per individual activity. Total work time = 3 minutes.

There are 2 x active exercises followed by 1 x static exercise per set.

<u>SET 1</u>   Sit ups, alternate ankle touches, static star, both sides

<u>SET 2</u>   Crunches – both arms, diagonal pushes, reverse static support both feet and elbows

Alternate Sets:

<u>ALT 1</u>   Through pushes, curl ups, static support on elbow and foot, both sides

<u>ALT 2</u>   Supine abdominal raising and lowering, supported by hands and heels, pronate abdominal raising and lowering, supported by hands and toes, static pronate support on forearms and toes.

Any of the above can be mixed into any combination.

Superman exercises, using either of the following two, or alternate on consecutive days:

<u>SM1</u>   Lie face down on floor, raise one limb off the ground by 6 inches and hold for set time. Start left arm, right arm, left leg, right leg. Next raise and hold 2 x limbs off the ground. Left arm and right leg, right arm and left leg, left arm and left leg, right arm and right leg, finally lift both arms and legs off the ground and hold for set time.

<u>SM2</u>   The second routine is to support yourself on all fours (both hands and knees). From this starting position, extend and raise out 1 x limb out straight and hold for set time. Start left arm, right arm, left leg, right leg, then 2 x limbs

simultaneously, left arm and right leg, right arm and left leg, then left arm and left leg, finally right arm and right leg.

Start by holding each position for 15 x seconds and then over time gradually increase the time to 30 x second holds.

To recap, use 2 of the sets (with 2 x active and 1 x static exercises) and then one of the superman routines.

The total maximum workout time is 3 minutes for the 2 x sets and 4 minutes for the superman set = 7 minutes daily.

Warm Up and Stretch Exercises

Warming up and cooling down are most important to the start and finish of the training session. It improves the level of performance during the exercise session and help accelerate the recovery process. Effectively you are reducing the muscle stiffness and help warm everything up before getting stuck into the more serious stuff.

In general Bill got us to use the rower to warm the body's temperature up on, although we did every now and then use a treadmill or cycle just to get off the ergo seat. Times differed on warming up before conducting stretching exercises, but were never less than 15 minutes for both warm up and cool down and towards the end we were up at 20-25 minutes. I once cycled down to the gym in Hereford from my village, a distance of about 7 miles and I was knackered before I started my main session and completely exhausted on my return home!

We had 2 x stretch programmes that alternated each day, and during the programme we would stretch off those muscle groups as we went through, for example, hamstrings, groins, quadriceps, achilles', shoulders, trunk lower back etc;

Programme A	Programme B
On back, two leg raise	Alternate leg sprints
Tuck jumps	Star jumps from squat to star
Press ups	Reverse dips on bench/box
Step ups on chair, stool knee height	Donkey kicks, out and return
Cycle crunches, alt elbow to alt knee	Sit ups, elbows to knees

Burpee's	Squat thrusts
Back arches, on tummy	Lateral leg lifts
Crunches on stool/chair	Alternate bench springs
Rebound line jumps	Trunk curls
Abdominal raise	Back raise
Heel raise	Hip flexors
Alt jumps, changing front foot on landing	Lunges, alt legs
Trunk rotation, with pole across shoulders	Side bends, both sides
Line touches	Skipping, with/without rope

Circuit Training

Two words describe this session – nasty business! Designed to inflict pain but also to simultaneously improve mobility, stamina and strength. We did a series of 8 x exercises (all in the gym but with imagination could be done outside as well) of which we were timed on each exercise, a short timed break, before moving onto the next. The duration on each exercise differed from week to week, and all exercises should be done at 100% effort. Ideally you need to have someone helping you here with a stopwatch and to encourage you to move to the next exercise. As the intensity builds the motivation to move from one exercise to the other weakens! It is also helpful for that other person with the stopwatch to record the number of repetitions completed so that new goals can be set for the next visit to purgatory!

The 8 x exercises were: Press ups, Squat thrusts, shuttle runs, star jumps, sit ups, bench dips, superman raise/back arches and alternate bench springs.

An example of the circuit timings are below:

Week	Work	Rest	No of Circuits	Rest between circuits
1	30 sec	30 sec	2	2 mins
2	40 sec	40 sec	2	2 mins
3	50 sec	50 sec	2	3 mins
4	30 sec	30 sec	3	2 mins
5	40 sec	40 sec	3	2 mins

6	50 sec	50 sec	3	3 mins
7	40 sec	40 sec	3	2 mins
8	30 sec	30 sec	3	2 mins

Weight Training Circuits:

Weights (all in kg's) are shown below:

Exercise	Wk 1	Wk 2	Wk 3	Wk 4
Bent Arm Rowing	20	21	22	18
Squat Front	20	21	22	18
Chest Press	63	65	70	58
Squat Back	25	26	27.5	20
Pullover	22	23	24	20
Power Cleans	20	21	22	18
Leg Extension	95	100	110	90
Leg Curl	95	100	110	90
Tricep Curl	38	39	40	36
Shoulder Press	45	48	50	40

Wk 1 3 sets x 3 reps,   Wk 2 3 sets x 4 reps,
Wk 3 3 sets x 5 reps,   Wk 4 3 sets x 3 reps.

Fartlek

Derived from the Swedish term that means 'Speed Play', Fartlek can provide an excellent endurance and strength session, as well as increase speed.

Our Fartlek training involving a number of repetitions on the same piece of equipment, in this case we used the ergo rowing trainer, Concept 2. Bill's goals for us for each week's session were as follows:

3 x mins easy, 2 x mins moderate and 1 x min hard – with 1 x minute rest between reps.

Week 1 = 10 reps, Week 2 = 11 reps, Week 3 = 12 reps, Week 4 = 8 reps.

Wild Waters in the Roar

Easy rowing was anything between 18- 26 SPM (strokes per minute) at around 2 min 12 seconds per 500m, Moderate was slightly faster at 20-26 SPM at around 2 mins per 500m, and finally Hard equated to 22-30 SPM at 1 min 55 seconds or less per 500m. After the 5th or 6th repetition this was hard work!

Row Sessions

In addition to those completed in the gym in accordance with Bill's programme, I had bought a fairly cheap indoor rower for use at home. This allowed me the option to complete some rowing on those days that I could not get to the gym. Before we got hands on TRANSVenture and took her out on the water, all our rowing was on Concept 2 machines, and I am utterly convinced that one has to do a lot of mileage on these beasts to be fit enough to seriously row an ocean. The fact that an ocean rowing boat and oars on the sea in no way behaves in the same manner, that you are being thrown off your seat and probably only one oar is biting into the water is neither here nor there when it comes to physical preparation. You must get on a Concept 2 regularly and put some miles in!

We always tried to set goals for the longer rows with SPM and distance covered so that we could always see improvements or not. Rob was a lot stronger on the ergo than me, and it was always with dread that I would admit my total distance for a session knowing that he was able to do a lot more. To start it made me feel inferior, but over time I got closer and closer to his standard, albeit never once did I better him on the ergo. However sessions had to be interesting otherwise they could be both mind blowing boring and very sore on the bottom! For example, in Week 3 of the programme below, my aim was to break down the 105 minutes into mini goals, primarily to set myself targets but also to relieve the boredom of sitting on the ergo. So, my goals for that session would be:

5 minutes at 20 SPM (WU phase),	@ 2:10 distance = 1153m
20 minutes at 22 SPM	@ 2:08 distance = 4966m
20 minutes at 22 SPM	@ 2:05 distance = 4979m
20 minutes at 24 SPM	@ 2:00 distance = 5000m
20 minutes at 24 SPM	@ 1:58 distance = 5084m

20 minutes at 22 SPM   @ 2:05 distance = 4979m
10 minutes at 20 SPM (CD phase)   @ 2:14 distance = 2238m

Total distance for session = 28,399m

Towards the end of our training we were regularly doing 2 and 3 hour rows, breaking for a couple of hours and then back to another 2 hours. It meant you had to have very understanding gym staff and wife, as often food had to be cooked at odd hours to accommodate my gym sessions!

The Training Programme

Here is an example of my programme for December 2002, with 4 months to go before starting the row. Robs is very similar except his weights are higher than mine. Each session would be preceded by warm up, stretch and core stability plus rowing squats (without weights). It looks 'busy' but it did work:

Training Programme Month of December 2002

	Week 1	Week 2	Week 3	Week 4
Day 1	Row Squats x 140	Row Squats x 150		Row Squats x 120
	WU – 15 mins easy row	WU – 15 mins jog	REST	WU 12 mins easy row
	Core Stab. & Stretch	Core Stab. & Stretch		Core Stab. & Stretch
	Weight Trg	Circuit Trg, 30 sec & 2		Weight Trg
	CD – 15 mins easy row	CD – 15 mins jog		CD – 12 mins easy row
Day 2	Row Squats x 140	Row Squats x 150	Row Squats x 160	Row Squats x 120
	Core Stab. & Stretch	WU – 18 mins easy row	WU – 20 mins jog	Core Stab. & Stretch
	Row 1hr 15 mins	Core Stab. & Stretch	Core Stab. & Stretch	Row 1 hr
	CD – Swim 14 mins	Weight Trg	Circuit Trg 50 sec x 3	CD Swim 12 mins
	any stroke	CD – 18 mins easy row	CD – 20 mins jog	any stroke
Day 3	Row Squats x 140	Row Squats x 150	Row Squats x 160	Row Squats x 120
	WU – 15 mins easy row	Row 1 hr 30 mins	Core Stab. & Stretch	Core Stab. & Stretch
	Core Stab. & Stretch	Row 1 hr 30 mins	Core Stab. & Stretch	Core Stab. & Stretch
	Weight Trg	CD Swim 16 mins	Weight Trg	Fartlek x 8 reps
	CD – 15 mins easy row	any stroke	CD – 20 mins row	CD – 12 mins swim

Day 4	Row Squats x 140	Row Squats x 150	Row Squats x 160	Row Squats x 120
	Core Stab. & Stretch	WU – 18 mins easy row	Core Stab. & Stretch	WU 12 mins easy row
	Row 3 mins hard x 10 reps	Core Stab. & Stretch	Row 1 hr 45 mins	Core Stab. & Stretch
	Row 3 mins easy x 10 reps	Weight Trg	CD Swim 20 mins	Weight Trg
	CD Swim 14 mins	CD – 18 mins easy row	any stroke	CD 12 mins easy row
Day 5	Row Squats x 140	Row Squats x 150	Row Squats x 160	Row Squats x 120
	WU – 15 mins easy row	WU – 18 min swim	WU – 20 mins row	Core Stab. & Stretch
	Core Stab. & Stretch	Core Stab. & Stretch	Core Stab. & Stretch	Row 3 mins hard x 9
	Weight Trg	Fartlek x 11 reps	Weight Trg	Row 3 mins easy x 9
	CD – 15 mins easy row	CD – 18 swim	CD 20 mins row	CD 12 mins swim
Day 6	Row Squats x 140		Row Squats x 140	
	WU – 15 mins swim	REST	Core Stab. & Stretch	REST
	Core Stab. & Stretch		Row 3 mins hard x 12 reps	
	Fartlek x 10 reps-		Row 3 mins easy x 12 reps	
	CD 15 mins swim		CD 20 mins swim	
Day 7	REST	Row Squats x 150	Row Squats x 160	Row Squats x 120
		WU – 18 mins easy row	WU - 20 mins jog	WU 12 mins easy row
		Core Stab. & Stretch	Core Stab. & Stretch	Core Stab. & Stretch
		Weight Trg	Fartlek x 12 reps	Weight Trg
		CD – 18 min easy row	CD – 20 mins jog	CD 12 mins easy row

Nutrition

What to eat, when and in what quantities were questions that soon raised their heads above the parapet, and needless to say we had no idea about the answers to any of them! So we went about doing some research and also gaining the advice from Bill Black who I turn put us onto nutritional experts at the University of Salford.

The UK Department of Health Estimated Average Requirement (EAR) for a daily intake of 2550 calories for men. Our advice was to eat closer to 6000 calories per day and to gain more weight

Protein is a building block for muscle. High protein foods include: chicken, lean meats, egg whites, turkey, tuna and other fish meat.

Mike Noel-Smith

    Until I started following a routine to eat, my gains were minimal. Once I set my eating times to a specific time during the day along with a protein boost, I could see the gains immediately.

Meal 1 - 6:00am
1 packet of a meal replacement with 16 ounces of skim milk
1 serving of whole grain cereal
1 cup of non/low-fat yogurt
1 piece of fruit

Meal 2 - 8:30am
1 serving of whey protein mixed in 10 ounces of water
1 large apple

Meal 3 -12:00pm
2 grilled chicken breasts
1 serving of brown rice
1 cup of low-fat yogurt
1 serving of whey protein

Meal 4 - 3:00pm
1 packet of a meal replacement with 16 ounces of water and 5-10 grams of L-Glutamine
1 large banana
Pre-Workout
1 workout bar

Meal 5 - 6:00pm (Post-workout)
1 serving of whey protein combined with 1 5gram serving of Creatine mixed in kool-aid.

Meal 6 -7:00pm
8 to 10 ounces of a lean round or flank steak
1 serving of rice
1 medium baked potato
1 large green salad

Meal 7 - 9:00pm
1 packet of a meal replacement with 16 ounces of skim milk
1 large banana
3 to 5 grams of L-Glutamine

When at sea our menu's were reasonable varied:
Chicken Curry with Rice
Beef and Potato Casserole
Spaghetti Bolognese
Boil in the Bag
Mushroom Risotto

*

APPENDIX 3
POEMS WE RECEIVED AT SEA

*

We Have Seen Creation…
Can any doubt the existence of a Creator
Who have shed their land bound living
And ventured upon the vast expanse of ocean?
Or failed to feel the awe of ancient cartographers
Who peopled it with strange & fearsome creatures…
Filling every corner with the whistling winds.
We've seen the sun rise and sink in matchless colours,
Felt its fiery strength throughout the day
And travelled cool, cocooned in starlight.
Unclouded by the haze of night-time townships
We saw the blood red planet in its orbit,
In a world illumined by the glow of phosphorescence.
Rowed with turtle in its leather coracle,
Been circled by sharks suspecting rivals,
Laughed aloud at flying fish at play.
Amazed at the abundance of the birdlife
When nearest land was deep beneath the sea,
Unfettered as they travelled aerial highways.
We have heard thunder rolling onwards
As lightening stabbed into the sea
The waters all around us boiling.
Flown, barely touching wave tops
As zephyrs blew their trumpets in our wake,
And slid us into troughs of deepest green.

Mike Noel-Smith

Then Triton thrashed war horses into fury,
Every wind from heaven blew our craft,
Rudderless, entirely helpless, they tossed us as a game.
As Jonah in the whale our call for help was heard,
And found, a pinpoint spinning in that ocean,
Survival only upmost in our minds.
In a nightmare of soaking, rolling darkness
Caring hands answered the seaman's code,
We like earth's first creatures crawled aboard.
Of course we regret that circumstances prevented
Our journey through planned points across the ocean,
When all our hopes and aims seemed to be lost.
But we have dared where others feared to venture,
We have experienced the awesome might of the Creator
Who in His gentle mercy brought us safely home.

Di Bagshawe

The Change's
Wind behind the vessel,
To the sides as well,
Taking them both forward
Safely as they go!

You behind are coping,
Somedays good, some not.
But strength is sent to
You, you know,
For many, many souls

A venture into the unknown,
That brings up lots of light.
A movement of the chackras
Emerging chunks of light

Wild Waters in the Roar

Some say that this is madness,
But spirits have to go,
And use their precious values,
For others to re-grow!

Your journey's will be different,
Sunshine, rain, will be,
Evident at times to you,
Sometimes you'll want to flee.
Bit at the end of this one,
The two of you will see,
The inner souls big message,
That your both meant to be!

Be connected souly,
Spirit hearts entwined,
New adventures showing,
The old you's left behind!

So as you start your journeys
I send you love and light,
To help you both discover,
Your hearts connect, that's right.

Entrust your spirits upwards,
Let loose your pain inside,
Don't hold onto emotions,
Let them loose and ride.

Ride your waves of learning,
Smooth your beings soul,
Health and happiness to you,
Love to both your souls.

Christina Morgan

Mike Noel-Smith

Peace
Deep peace of the running wave to you
Deep peace of the burning air to you
Deep peace of the quiet earth to you
Deep peace of the shining stars to you
Deep peace of the Son of peace to you

Iona

To sea
"Father, the ocean is so large
My boat is so small…
Watch over me"

Breton fisherman's prayer

The Secret of the Sea
My soul is full of longing
For the secret of the sea,
And the heart of the great ocean
Sends a thrilling pulse through me

Longfellow

Printed in the United Kingdom
by Lightning Source UK Ltd.
133060UK00003B/178-441/P